THE BANKRUPT CIRCUS & OTHER MISADVENTURES

THE BANKRUPT CIRCUS & OTHER MISADVENTURES

J. BRADLEY MINNICK

PRAISE FOR J. BRADLEY MINNICK

THE BANKRUPT CIRCUS

LOVE this! Love the crazed miraculous whacky magical OMG style. Pure genius. Thank you for sending me over the moon with "The Bankrupt Circus." Nobody writes fiction like this. Nobody. 🧡

—JO MCDOUGALL, FORMER ARKANSAS POET LAUREATE, AUTHOR OF *IN THE HOME OF THE FAMOUS DEAD* AND *TOWNS FACING RAILROADS*

WORKING THE DIRT

To read Brad Minnick's fiction is to enter a world of alternative, diminished lives, places any of us could have ended up in except for the grace of a higher being. A world of "Sad Lives" and "Secret Selves." Of librarians named Stipend, and principals named Whorl. Of janitors unable to comprehend baseball and whose only real friend is their Mighty Broom. Yet, like any genuinely higher being, Minnick loves even the least of his creations, dignifying them with an empathy and a beauty of purpose that leaves the reader both stunned and uplifted.

—JOHN VANDERSLICE, AUTHOR OF *ISLAND FOG* AND *LAST DAYS OF OSCAR WILDE*

GENERATIVE/ITERATIVE/EVALUATIVE

This story is head-spinning, mind-twisting, yet has a complete inner logic. Minnick offers a humble human moment and with a combination of comedy and supple linguistics, elevates it to a bird-eye view of the (or a) human condition. In the words of Ferdinand de Saussure, "In practice, the study of language is in some degree or other the concern of everyone."

—JOHNNY PAYNE, AUTHOR OF *A GRAVEYARD OF FIRST CHAPTERS*, AND *HARD SIDE OF THE RIVER*

A PEBBLE AT DAWN

In "A Pebble at Dawn," as in the many other fine stories in his debut collection, J. Bradley Minnick reveals himself to be one part William Saroyan, one part Groucho Marx, with a joke on his tongue and a thousand hearts in his hands. He sees truly but slyly, that is to say, the kind of writer who gazes into people's souls while pretending he's looking the other way.

—KEVIN BROCKMEIER, AUTHOR OF *A BRIEF HISTORY OF THE DEAD* AND *THE ILLUMINATION*

THE LAST TELEGRAPH

"The Last Telegraph" is a story about the distances between fathers and sons, about all the frequencies we transmit on, and about the moment we finally speak in our own voice. Set amid suburban decorum, where a boy shouts himself voiceless every afternoon and neighbors flee with stammered excuses, it asks: How do we learn to decode ourselves, to find some essential core and telegraph it back to reality? In his father's den, young William discovers that the deepest conversations happen in silence, that we inherit our parents' frequencies, and that being heard requires first learning to listen. This is a story about the long education of the heart—about what we lose and what we find when words finally fail us.

— WILLIAM LYCHACK, WINNER OF THE PUSHCART PRIZE AND AUTHOR OF *THE WASP EATERS* AND *THE ARCHITECT OF FLOWERS*

"Lady ears! Love the whacky ping-pong repartee when the old lady shows up."

—Stewart O'Nan, author of A Prayer for the Dying and Last Night at the Lobster

"Clean Up in the Meat Dept."

For Mom & Dad

CONTENTS

Artwork Credits

Karen Rile — Artwork created for *The Bankrupt Circus*. Artwork is reproduced with the artist's permission.

Ryan Scribner — Artwork created for *Nobody Beats Vitas Gerulaitis 17 Times in a Row*. Artwork is reproduced with the artist's permission.

L.K. Sukany — Artwork created for *The Twisted S*; *Fly Stand, Inquire Herein*; *Innocently to Amuse the Imagination in this Dream of Life is Wisdom*; *Notes From Tennis Camp*; *The Last Telegraph*. All artwork is reproduced with the artist's permission.

THE BANKRUPT CIRCUS

Before the Bankrupt Circus came to town, my bud, Decie, and I spent our summer lunch breaks arguing about the merits of olive loaf sandwiches while we sat on the curb in the midst of chores in front of his mother's house—a squat typical one-story brick affair—two eleven-year-old boys caught in the grip of the summer lunch-time economic blahs.

Remember olive loaf? It's a working man's lunch meat: one-part salty bologna, one-part salty olives, a third-part salty preservatives—a super salty concoction that went down perfectly with cold orange sodas in pull-tab cans.

Thus, during our lunch breaks, Decie and I found ourselves embroiled in arguments about the merits of proper condiments. It was difficult for me to agree with what my bud, Decie, said, even when the bold and ludicrous statements that verily fell from his salt-encrusted tongue turned out to be true. We were both in perfect agreement, however, that mustard added a layer of sticky brine to the meat; ketchup was just plain gross; combinatorial spread mixtures sat too heavy, even on an eleven-year-old belly; heretofore, Decie boldly stated that only a cool layer of mayo spread deliciously atop the part-olive, part-meat would do—I opted for Miracle Whip.

"Expeller Pressed Organic Soybean Oil, then," Decie smirked.

"Low-fat whipped cottage cheese," I gagged.

We both stuck our fingers down our throats at the mention of low-fat.

Decie and I argued for a while longer and then

turned to the importance of bread—we both agreed individual hoagie rolls purchased from Benvenuti's Market on the corner were essential and far better than the crusty stuff in the Bread Depot. Benvenuti and his babushka-wearing wife, Carm, baked fresh bread on Fridays. I argued that Friday's rolls were fresher; Decie argued that Saturday's rolls gained in experience.

Then, Decie's mother stuck her head out the door and pointed to the lawn mower, the gutters on the roof, the hose in the yard, and the paint cans next to the door.

As I said, until the Bankrupt Circus came to town, arguments about the merits of olive loaf, the most lubricating condiments, and the best day for purchasing bread had been the cultural capital of our summer vacation—as much ado about anything and everything as nothing at all.

Enter: Decie's neighbor—Mr. Rancer.

For every day of the year save one, the summer solstice—the longest day of the year—Mr. Rancer refused to allow anyone to set foot on his perfect grass. Neighborhood boys, almost grown, heads filled with the unpleasant and humiliating memories of being lectured to and berated by Mr. Rancer in his Economics class, spent their nights rambling through the middle of his yard. This intrepid battle raged on until Mr. Rancer literally raised the stakes, knocking spiky metal heads into the ground and, through cause and effect, tore Tommy Tutonie's oil pan right out from the bottom of his car. All Mr. Rancer had to do was follow the oil leak up the street and write down the license plate number. Afterwards, Mr. Rancer's KEEP OFF THE GRASS sign became a permanent fixture, except on the longest day of the year when he took it down and put up another to promote his garage sale, thus letting all trod on his beloved grass.

As far as I could tell, Mr. Rancer imagined himself the middleman of garage sales. In late spring he frequented them most weekends, when he wasn't tending to his lawn, bought the most unusual items, and then waited for his fortunes to improve by staging his own super-saver-summer-solstice garage sale blow-out. That's what his sign said anyway. Problem was, when it came time to resell the junk, Mr. Rancer never remembered quite how much he had originally paid, and he never put price tags on anything. Each time one tried to hand him money, he insisted on haggling for both fun and profit.

Mr. Rancer would wait for an offer and then begin right away to drive up the price. "Simple supply and demand," he would say. "You'd know this, Decie, if you ever had the G's to ante up and take macro-economics. Simple liquidity, son. The beauty of the free market at work right here in the ol' neighborhood."

"The two miniature unicycles," Mr. Rancer told me, "had belonged to The Bankrupt Circus, and they had only been ridden by clowns—not bear cubs." Rancer said he "picked 'em up for a song. The Bankrupt Circus," he explained, "had gone belly-up and stalled just outside of Hiemont." Bank officials, Rancer told me, had seized nearly everything, and when it was clear the Bankrupt Circus would forever be insolvent, officials began selling off items in lots.

Immediately, I could tell Mr. Rancer regretted that he had tipped his hat and whispered, "Nick, let's just keep these little particulars between you and me, okay?" Along with the unicycles, Rancer bought flashy fringed costumes worthy of tightrope walkers and trapeze artists, and he displayed these costumes all along the concrete walls of his garage. Additionally, he had procured a human cannon, two whips (he refused to sell these to children—said he was going to "use 'em on anyone who stepped on his grass"), two giant spheres (you could climb into them and roll around), and three hoops he lectured "an enterprising performer could light on fire and juggle."

For weeks that June, we had seen unemployed circus performers hanging around Hiemont's town limits with their animals—monkeys in military vests and caps, tiny pigs in summer dresses, and bear cubs wearing spiked collars—waiting for the 51C bus.

A photographer for The Hiemont Chronicle snapped a photo exposé, posing the down-and-out Strongman, an unkempt bearded woman, a flaccid Muscles the Clown, and a tattooed fire-eater holding the ends of the leashes attached to the befuddled animals, who in the pictures looked forlorn, sick, and down in-the-mouth.

Such stories usually go unnoticed, but this one, perhaps because of its high pathos, caught fire, and before Hiemont could issue "damage control," our best local newsman, Yippie Freeman, was busy interviewing the Bankrupt Circus performers.

The following statement was issued to Yippie by Muscles the Clown on KUKY: "When a clown, willing and humble, can't get work in America, the whole meritocracy is DEAD!" Muscles the Clown was, of course, alluding to a whole way of life that had, in fact, been taken away when those multinational corporations had moved in right next to so many of Hiemont's independent mom-and-pop stores. Places like the Bread Depot.

On television, the circus performers were not drunk—although no one would have blamed them had they been. Instead, they used their wits and innate understanding of the entertainment news capital America was becoming—all an illusion—and they grabbed the big fat ill-fitting keys to even the most cynical grown-up child's heart.

Muscles the Clown, because of his facility with Standard English, quickly became the spokesman for the group of cast-out circus performers, all of whom decided exactly when it was best to let go of their leashes.

CBS broke the story nationally, and twenty million viewers tuned in. Each night, experts sounded off and provided multi-screened commentary underneath sad pictures. The Town of Hiemont was forced to issue an unremorseful apology for closing down the circus and trying bit by bit to sell it off. Nobody believed the town officials' apologies, and this disbelief turned America irate and further stoked the viral ether.

"In America," Muscles the Clown said, "a half-assed apology is worse than no bleeping apology at all." Twenty million viewers didn't even move to cover their children's ears, nor was there the expected outrage over Muscles the Clown's poor and un-calibrated statement. Even eleven-year-olds like us recognized that Muscles the Clown had spoken from his real, not his rubber heart.

He was a person underneath that painted-on clown smile—after all.

Thankfully, I was able to haggle with Mr. Rancer for the unicycles before Show BIZ TV got whoopee-cushioned wind, flatulent and fetid, of the capitalistic unpleasantness going down in that bargain-basement garage sale across town.

On television, Rancer looked apoplectic, pointing and making great and pronounced finger gestures in the direction of the BIZ TV's news truck tires that had found purchase in his front lawn. "Doesn't a man have any rights? Isn't anything sacred?" Rancer howled red-faced into three different cameras while attempting to hurl a circus ball through the windshield of the news truck— the same circus ball, we later learned, that had spent most of its time encircled in the trunk of a well-worn and beloved elephant named FRIEDA, who preened and balanced and raced for The Cure. (YouTube showed footage of Freida extending an uncoiling trunk, snooted around a large-sized check for a sizable amount to thankful wig-wearing children, thus inflating several Big Top towns all across America.)

Yippie Freeman reported, "In this downtrodden economy with so many homeless and unemployed, there is something about the desperate pieces of this story that has found its way pluckily into the main artery of America's heartstrings. A Bankrupt Circus, dehydrated animals, and now an unemployed Muscles the Clown [backlit picture of Muscles flexing inverted arms] put a face on the problem."

Public television pontificated: "Picture yourself,

standing there, holding the end of a forlorn leash, attached to an unhappy bear cub named Bubby. The animals, the clowns, and America are in bondage, and those of us who pay attention clearly realize Muscles' painted-on smile is the same smile we put on every morning. And, those of us who truly do care to reflect for even the shortest amount of time on this America, our America, realize that we are all down-and-out clowns; we are all pitiable circus animals attached to leashes, and we can't let go because we have held onto them for so long that we have come to believe they are extensions of our arms. Has America, as represented by this tiny northern town, turned into a Bankrupt Circus?"

And then, when the President, in an off-hand remark, referred to evidence of a "Bankrupt Circus" after pointing to a series of boarded-up financial institutions, those in the media suffered a veritable viral parapraxis. Quickly added to pop culture's idiomatic urban dictionary—The Bankrupt Circus came to mean more than "I sincerely apologize."

Luckily, though, while America was seemingly at a standstill, Decie and I had bought, paid for, and wheeled away two shiny Bankrupt Circus unicycles shortly before Biz TV's heavy news truck sullied Mr. Rancer's lawn, and he became known as "The Grass Crank from Hiemont."

Decie and I didn't give a shit about the news; we didn't read any newspapers, and although big events— usually celebrity deaths found their way to us later rather than sooner—in truth, we didn't care either way. We had more important things to argue about—the merits of olive loaf and figuring out how to ride those one-wheeled bicycles I had blown my birthday money on.

Decie grabbed a unicycle from my hands, ran astride of it, and attempted to hop onto the banana-shaped seat, as if he were an outlaw pulling himself up onto a galloping horse; he sat atop the seat for a few painful seconds, howled in a high-pitched falsetto and fell to the ground, gently cupping his nads. He yelled, "My balls have become bruised olives," which brought to mind our constant arguments about olive loaf sandwiches and put me in no mood, I assure you, to eat them. Decie found his unsteady feet. He was still nursing his injuries. I prayed he wasn't going to ask me to take a look.

Aside from being nearly maimed, Decie was convinced that we had been gypped, and he insisted that we return the unicycles—invoking the Lemon Law.

Hell, I was trying to do a good thing, something different, you know?

By the time we wheeled the unicycles back to Rancer's house, the BIZ TV truck had set its tires permanently on his once-pristine lawn, and Mr. Rancer's comments were being edited into usable sound bites; there was footage of him hitting Yippie Freeman over the head with his big-super-saver-summer-solstice garage sale blow-out sign, stealing Freeman's handheld microphone, and spewing forth the following: "One of the consequences of such notions as 'entitlements' is that people who have contributed nothing to society feel that society owes them something, apparently just for being nice enough to grace us with their presence." [1] We last saw Mr. Rancer using the circus whip repeatedly on the BIZ TV truck tires before being wrestled to the ground and led away in handcuffs. "Arrested," Rancer's snarky lawyer said, "humiliated, disgraced, taken away from his own garage sale. Just a poor American man trying to make a buck."

Decie and I quickly learned on that summer solstice day that all wasn't quite as it appeared when an inexorable gaggle of clowns from the Bankrupt Circus suddenly replaced the haggling Mr. Rancer with wide-angled, make-up-smeared shots of tear-filled clown faces reunited with their beloved costumes, juggle rings, cherry noses, fake ears and pairs of floppy shoes.

There is that now infamous picture of Muscles the Clown, who stands in his polka dotted socks pointing with wonder and reunited with his bulbous shoes, the laces of which dangle by a nail pounded into the block cement with a sign that read, "Best Offer."

Muscles the Clown points to his hammer-toed feet and says, I quote, "We thought everything, even our shoes, had been sold off and were long, long gone, but it's all here!"

While Mr. Rancer was presumably being finger-printed, Muscles the Clown and his ilk took over his garage and, in full view of all, and on cable television, performed a spontaneous, first-ever to America's knowledge, Garage Sale Circus—the idea being if they could collect enough money, maybe, just maybe, they could pay their debtors, buy back their circus stuff and reverse the insolvency that had injected itself into the content of the American character.

Enter: Decie, all bruised and holding his balls, and

me with a huge smile—as if we had recently got wind of the Garage Sale Circus and, on cue, were returning the unicycles we had ourselves wrested away from a rich neighborhood capitalist and were wheeling them back to their rightful owners.

"Everything must go!" Muscles the Clown shouted.

As we rolled the unicycles into the garage, Yippie Freeman, now in a flak jacket and with an icepack on his head, said: "There are glimmers in the boyhood of America that with steadfast prayer and a belief that if just given a chance, our younger generation will rise to the occasion, if called so forth."

This made-up back-story, without a word to deny it, confirmed what everyone perched by a television set in America was thinking.

"Their Quixotic quest is over!" Muscles the Clown reiterated and pointed a stiff finger at us.

Suddenly, all of the clowns surrounded us and were patting us on the heads and rubbing our bellies and going, "Bong! Bong! Bong!"

"And now ladies and germs, what's a Garage Sale Circus without—animals!"

Enter: three seals who tossed beach balls with their noses and bear cubs still wearing collars, who rolled around with purpose on the insides of hollow spheres.

"We wish we had the elephants, but alas all the elephants, even Freida, have been impounded. Help save the elephants!" Muscles the Clown again pointed his flaccid finger at America.

A strongman appeared wheeling out the human

cannon, which came to a grinding halt before us, and Muscles gestured like clowns do for Decie to "Get in."

Decie, overcome by the moment, hesitated.

"This is NOT a good idea," I said but my voice was drowned out by an orchestra of fun whistles and stupid kazoos.

I saw the last of Decie's head disappear into the mouth of the cannon.

Then, the Fire Eater appeared as if from the very walls of Mr. Rancer's garage and pulled from his mouth a flaming sword, which still had the price tag on it, which he used to light the comically enormous cannon's fuse.

"Ten-nine-eight," Muscles the Clown began the count, "seven-six-five" we all chimed in "four-three-two" BOOM!—a thousand leaflets burst from the human cannon like confetti, advertising the Garage Sale Circus. Muscles the Clown made a big 'to-do' about climbing onto the barrel with a handheld camera and peering down into the mouth of the human cannon.

"The boy is nowhere to be found!" Muscles the Clown exclaimed and pushed his gloved hands to the side of his face.

[Wide-angle of the impossibly empty barrel.]

"Gone to free the elephants," Muscles exclaimed and clasped his hands together like a supplicant.

The kazoos crescendoed and the fun whistles shrieked, and then everything about the Garage Sale Circus paused— "Commercial," the Bearded Lady whispered in my ear as soft as silk.

The clowns suddenly grabbed the unicycles from my hands.

Five minutes later, the annoying kazoos and ear-splitting fun whistles started up again; errant clowns were hopping on pogos, two bear cubs were riding the unicycles, and there was Muscles the Clown still sitting astride the cannon, a camera lens very close to his face, "And ladies and germs, theeerrrreeee he is!" The flaccid finger suddenly turned straight.

Decie made his way from around the side of the garage—leading five elephants trunk-to-tail in tow. "They follow the boy like butter," Muscles the Clown said into the camera while behind him the elephants put on a show: they balanced on little stools, they tossed bouncy balls back and forth, they tilted their great hoary heads and trumpeted in the air freedom's sounds upon command.

Re-enter: the Fire Eater who held up a large ring aflame. I tasted the creosote and smoke.

The cub bears were holding hands, balancing their furry bottoms atop the unicycles. Together they gathered up speed and jumped through the flaming ring, over three tiny pigs, and landed successfully on God's side, our side.

One cub bear dismounted, and there was Decie in the middle of it all, clapping, happy.

I had never seen Decie so happy. When one of the clowns during the next commercial break showed him how to mount the unicycle, one foot on the ground, the other on the pedal and up! up! up! he grinned from ear to freckled ear. The Strongman and Muscles held onto each of his arms and together yelled, "The boy is on his way!"

As I stood there surrounded by clowns and bears and

elephants, as I watched the cannon being lit once more and advertisements and confetti being shot into the air —all I could think was, this whole thing should have happened to me. I was the one who bought the unicycles; I was the one who wheeled them back here; I was the one who understood cause and effect, supply and demand, the warp and the woof. Yet, it was sad-sac, ever-antagonizing Decie they had picked, not me.

I sat right down on the curb, I swear, and one of the 24-hour news guys handed me a sandwich, and guess what? It was olive loaf. Yet there was only mustard, not mayo, not Miracle Whip. And he said, "Kid, have you ever seen anything the likes of this?"

WORKING THE DIRT

Mighty Broom left the first notch in the dirt at three that afternoon: the first of hundreds of parallel lines exactly five feet apart across the width of the halls that started in front of the Janitors Closet and ran the length of Weatherspeake High. Wilson never had to measure the rows. He had the five-foot knack.

Twelve o'clock, midnight was quitting time. Wilson never looked forward to quitting time because then he had to go home to his mother, who loved him more than anything else in the world and was all smothery and lonesome and insisted on giving him five pats and five hugs and five kisses for luck before he went to bed.

Carl, his boss, was nice enough to let him take Mighty Broom home for the weekend. "Keep that dirty thing out on the porch," his mother always said, but she didn't really mean it.

Wilson usually went upstairs to his room and turned

on Mr. Train that ran like a subway around and under his bed and through his collection of pop cans that lined the walls and made a strange, shadowed city he wished he could visit in his dreams.

He would try to stay awake and watch the part of the city where the baseball stadium was, but when he fell asleep, the city stayed shadows, and only his mother appeared. "Goodnight Wilson," she said and kissed him once more on the forehead. Later, he sneaked out to the porch and rescued Mighty Broom and leaned it against his bedroom wall and put a shadowed wig on the city.

On Saturday, his mother took him on the subway train to a Phillies game. The subway tunnel was dark and scary and filled with unhappy ghosts. At the stadium, he bought a program for a dollar. While the game was going on, Wilson saw a young boy sitting in the row in front of him, making marks with a pencil on a page in the program. Wilson puzzled over the blank scorecard in his program and the symbols at the bottom of the page. "Do you want mustard on your hot pretzel?" Wilson's mother asked.

Wilson spent most of Sunday making signs on large rolls of paper while his mother sat in front of the television. "I'm knitting my will," she said. Before he could complete the signs, his mother always fell asleep.

"Finished!" Wilson yelled.

The signs were for sports teams that had to play the next week at Weatherspeake High. He hung them all around the gym: 'Boys Football, Wilson wishes you victory.' 'Girls Basketball—Wilson wishes you Wins.'

'Boys Wrestling—Wilson Wishes You Well.' 'Girls Volley-ball—Wilson Sends Well Wishes.' He felt proud when he shifted the words around because that made them matter more.

Monday morning he said to his mother, "Friday's forever and a day away." Tuesday he said to Principal Whorl, "Friday's more than two days and another day away!" Wednesday he said to Carl, "Friday's comin', day after tomorrow." Thursdays he said to himself, "Friday's comin', be here soon."

Thursday night, while he was sweeping up the library, he borrowed a book of baseball stories. It was the first time that Wilson had ever taken anything from the school that really counted. All the teachers talked about how books really counted, not like the candy for the taking in the glass jars on their desks or the half-empty pop cans sitting on the heater vents or the food in the refrigerators.

"That's stealing, Wilson," his mother would have said, and Wilson knew that it was stealing, but called it "borrowing," the same way the kids did. Wilson hid the baseball storybook under his jacket so his mother wouldn't know and went directly to his room.

That night, he kept score of the stories he read. The players never played full innings and, after a while, he could never tell which inning the players were in at all. Wilson realized that baseball stories weren't about base-ball in the same way that stealing wasn't about "borrow-ing" and pop cans weren't about cities. "God bless you, Wilson. Go to sleep now."

That night Wilson had dreams that Principal Whorl called him down to the Front Office over the big voice box in the ceiling. Everyone knew the principal was calling because Wilson was a "no-good stealer."

While he sat in one of the chairs that he always ran Pete The Sweeper under, the pretty secretary went "Tsk, Tsk, Tsk, Wilson!" Principal Whorl stood straight and tall at his door and was holding out his hand, palm up. Wilson smiled and tried to give him a high five, but Mr. Whorl slapped him in the face.

Wilson woke up all sweaty and felt like he was about to throw-up or Mr. P.P. Tinkle on the floor. He grabbed the baseball storybook that he had carefully hidden behind the shadowed city and shoved it way down in his workpants.

Friday morning, Wilson felt terrible and nervous. The butterflies had been at him all night. He had a strict schedule he was expected to follow. His boss, Carl, a red-faced man, yelled at him because he loved him so much. "Now listen, Wilson, I hand-printed the schedule and put it on the wall of the cafeteria. It's here every night now! This is where to look!" The schedule was printed in pencil because sometimes Carl needed to make changes.

Work time usually passed quickly, and Wilson kept himself busy. Besides, he had Pete The Sweeper, his not-so-trusty vacuum cleaner, to keep him company. Pete The Sweeper always trailed behind, its nozzle attached to his belt and noisily whispered, "Borrow the baseball book; nobody will miss it," while Wilson was in the library, or it vacuumed, "Eat the colorful candy from the pretty secretary's desk, Wilson. She likes you" while he was cleaning up the Front Office, or it screeched, "Food is in refrigerators" while he was in the cafeteria looking at Carl's hand-printed schedule, or it scraped, "There's a valuable pop can sitting on one of the drafting tables in the shop room; take it, Wilson. Just take it."

Mighty Broom was another story. It never interrupted him when he spoke like Carl or his mother or Principal Whorl. It walked in front of him down the halls, and he obediently followed. It told him which teachers were in the building, and if Mr. Whorl was there late; most of all, it worked the dirt in parallel lines exactly five feet apart, leaving doubts about the dirtiness of dirt.

"You look like a boy who's lost his marbles somewhere in his pockets and is trying to find them," Carl gave Wilson the ups-and-downs. "Why are you standing on one leg, Wilson? You gotta' pinch a loaf?" Carl's big eyeballs bulged, and his face got even redder like when he drank the "Night Train" behind the dumpsters on cold nights.

At six o'clock, Mighty Broom found its way into the theatre. The students were busy practicing for their latest production, moving about on the stage, saying their lines, and the lights were flashing colors that hurt Wilson's eyes. He was fascinated by the auditorium that was painted to look like the big city with skyscrapers, roads and a tunnel for a subway train. Wilson stood in front of the tunnel. Mighty Broom stopped but Pete The Sweeper trailed along behind and whispered, "Listen, Wilson. There's a train coming. I can hear it. You better hurry, or you'll be late."

At seven o'clock, Mighty Broom stopped in front of room 11. Gim Truit, the senior History teacher, had spent thirty years of his life in this room. "This room is *my* history, Wilson," Mr. Truit said. Mr. Truit was old and often sick.

Wilson knew there were two types of teachers at Weatherspeake High: Sad Lives and Secret Selves.

Sad Lives took their work home with them on weekends the same way that he took Mighty Broom home. They always talked about the school and told Wilson the same stories again and again. They stayed late on Fridays and came in on weekends. They went to all of the sporting events: sold tickets and soda and candy and disappeared at half-time and spent the remaining hours alone in their rooms. They complained, "Students take and take, Wilson, and they rarely give back. I'm flat-out empty."

Wilson knew that Sad Lives loved to complain and wouldn't have it any other way. They would always be sad.

The other type had Secret-Selves locked in a deep place and far away that no one could see. Secret Selves spent a lot of time away from the school and rarely worked late. They took long trips during the summers. They didn't want to become imprisoned in the pictures in the trophy case or to become ghosts destined to roam the halls; when they finally went away for good, they never came back for a visit, ever. They didn't even send postcards.

Mr. Truit was so old that students called him Plato because he had read every book in the Weatherspeake

Library. He told Wilson that he had to go into the army to fight the Korean War. He told Wilson that the Korean War was one of the bloodiest wars that had ever been fought. He told Wilson that the history books said that it hadn't even been a war but that the history books were wrong. "Blood flowed like a river onto the battlefield, Wilson." Wilson could see that river of blood and men being swept away, sinking down under the red waves. "Now listen, Wilson. Listen to me like your life depended on it. Listen to me because there's a war on, son—a war with our secret selves—a war with time."

Mr. Truit pointed to all of the paintings, sculptures and posters that lined his room. "This *represents* history, Wilson. But, it *isn't* history, don't you see?" Wilson shook his head. "Of course you do! Look, I know you understand. I watch you read that dirt. I know *your* secret."

It was then that the baseball book let loose and slipped all the way down his pants, and when Wilson shook his leg, the book flew out and hit the floor. "I tried to wish it away to but it let loose anyway," he apologized to Mr. Truit. Wilson quickly swept up the baseball book with Mighty Broom.

"There's more history in that dirt than all those books put together, isn't there, Wilson? Why you can tell more about all of us than we know about ourselves. You understand the dirt. You measure it into what matters." Mr. Truit's voice pushed Wilson and Mighty Broom and the baseball storybook down the hall.

Friday, eight o'clock was Wilson's favorite time. At eight o'clock, he swept the gym. Wilson had wanted to sweep it from the first day. Carl had said, "Wilson, sweeping gym floors is the most responsible job of all. You got to take care not to scratch the varnish. And for Christ's sake, don't leave the water fountain button on after you take your whale-sized drinks. Then, we'll both be up a crick without a paddle."

Alone with Mighty Broom, Wilson swept the gym's varnished floorboards and listened to Julie Andrews sing Christmas music over the voice box in the ceiling, even when it wasn't near Christmas. The old record bounced merrily through its grooves on the beat-up stereo that came down out of the wall, and music washed over his head.

Wilson always stopped in the dead-middle of the gym floor and admired his signs. "You been staring at them walls for fifteen minutes, Wilson. You'd think there was a picture of Miss U.S.A. hanging up there instead of your crummy signs," Carl said.

At 9 o'clock, the hallways of Weatherspeake High were filled with the ghosts of students come and gone. As Wilson swept past the trophy case, he always stopped to look at the pictures of all of the children smiling at the camera. Once in a while, they came back to visit but that was usually only after the first year. Sometimes they came back after a long time, and Wilson called them by name as if they had never left. They always looked amazed that someone remembered them.

"Them years coming faster; they's gaining on the future, but by then I'll be dead and you'll be gone, too," Carl said at least once a week. "Each year we get older, and each year the students stay the same," Mr. Whorl said on alternate weeks. "I heard that in a movie, Wilson, and it's stuck with me." Pete The Sweeper whispered, "Keep the colored pencils you find on the art tables, Wilson. Nobody notices strays." Mighty Broom admonished, "Keep sweeping, Wilson. Pay them no mind. We both plan to be around forever."

It was eleven o'clock, and Mighty Broom hurried Wilson through the dark halls, startling all of the ghosts who lurked in the corners. Together they all passed the Front Office and stopped at the front doors. Wilson shook the lock three times and said, "Lock, lock, locked."

Mighty Broom entered the library, and Wilson laid the baseball storybook he had borrowed on the floor and marveled as Mighty Broom scooted through the library with a mind of its own and swept the baseball storybook back onto bottom shelf so that nobody, not even Mrs. Stipend, the mean librarian, or Mr. Whorl, the Principal, or Carl, his boss, or his mother would know that he had once borrowed what counted, if only for a little while.

When the day he tried to wish away finally came to an end. He squatted down next to Mighty Broom and said to that last slash mark in the dirt, "I tried to wish it away, but here it is anyway." He said to Pete The Sweeper, "Friday's here. Be good in the Janitors Closet and don't borrow anything anyone will notice."

Wilson opened wide the Janitors Closet door to put Pete The Sweeper inside. To his surprise, on the shelf next to the paper towels he found a library book, *The History of Baseball,* with a note. "Wilson, I thought you could take care of this book for me over the weekend and return it to library on Monday. I borrowed it and didn't want the students and the teachers of Weatherspeake

High to miss it. Your Friend in History and otherwise, Mr. Truit."

At twelve o'clock, midnight, Wilson heard the choo-choo train on its way out of Weatherspeake, its horn echoing through the midnight air.

NOBODY BEATS
VITAS GERULAITIS
17 TIMES IN A ROW

I had saved up all last year to buy the Snauwaert. I loved the feel of it, and the red and blue and white. It offered me so much more than my older brother Barry's standard Jack Kramer racquet, which was chunky and, well, standardized—as if tennis was baseball—and the Kramer was boxlike, like my older brother. Barry was 17 and thought that anyone should be able to play tennis in Chucks with stalwart forbearance.

Shoes mattered, too. Shoes probably should have mattered the most, and yet, because they were so expensive—one had to make due with all-court treads, which though reliable on any surface weren't particularly useful on any either. Jimbo, Mac, Borg, and Vitas knew better than to take shoes for granted. Shoes were their meal ticket—especially through endorsements—and although one could only wear one pair at a time, it sure must have been nice to have so many from which to choose.

Strings—well, there was gut and none of us—even the country clubbers—had the scratch to keep us in gut. Plus, because of the unpredictability of the Pittsburgh weather, gut took way too much care.

I wore my blond hair like my hero, Vitas Gerulaitis. Vitas, notorious playboy, rolled to tennis matches in a gold Rolls Royce, couldn't be beaten by Jimmy Connors seventeen times in row and said as much—pushed himself with dogged determination.

Vitas, maybe if #1 and #2 and #3 weren't your friends, you would have been the best, but #4 suited you. The pressure was on, and the Snau set you off. Jimbo played with the Wilson T-2000—steel that very nearly vibrated into your soul. Johnny Mac's wooden Dunlop Maxply was a beast at the net.

I coveted tennis racquets—loved the feel of the different ones in my hands—begged my mother to take me to Tennis Haus so that I could examine the racquets that were carefully squeezed in between wooden dividers—not hanging from hooks and facing the customers like in the big box stores—where all that mattered about a racquet was if you could see it and balance it on your nose. Those box store racquets I had convinced myself were strictly for Sunday use with the croakers.

Borg used two racquets—the Donnay—sleek and small-headed, strung to 90 lbs. in Europe, and the Bankcroft Borg for the US Open, which he had never won. Borg's Bankcroft was chunky black, but the grip could be easily doubled up on. It was not light, and it was unwieldy at the net—not as unwieldy as Wilson's T-2000, which was uncontrollable and designed for max damage.

The T-2000 was a metal beast, with coils wrapped around the head as if to reinforce destruction. The ball pinged, ricocheting off the strings like it had hit a trampoline. There was no using it at the net because it felt like you were wielding a sword. This racquet was not for the meek but for the loud and brash. It did not have a sensitive side.

The Dunlop Maxply was oddly sleek and actually beautiful, with its various shades of wood, the laminates seamlessly glued together. It was a practical work of art, and one could do most anything with it, slice and dice, cut and spin, serve and volley. Its longevity in the back-court, however, could not be sustained. It was for subtlety and manipulation.

Then, there was the Snau: Three-toned, laminated, sleek headed, poised, slender, well-balanced, perfect. I outfitted my Snau with cool-blue specked nylons that made a "ping" and terrycloth grips, just like Vitas, who could wrap a grip in record speed during a changeover. I used old washcloths that my patient mother sewed over the leather with a needle and thread.

During my 14th year, I borrowed Barry's beloved Jack Kramer Autograph, which was heavy as hell, and during an autumn pick-up game, the bulky thing slipped out of my sweaty palm and came head-to-face with the pave-ment—and the racquet cracked. It was still playable, but Barry was steamed. He thought I was screwing around again and had let go of his Kramer on purpose. He pretty much accused me of throwing it down on the court just to spite him. Barry asked to borrow my beloved Snau for doubles with the croakers one Sunday morning. I pretty much had to concede, but I waited, sat on my hands, until he returned home in a bad mood, disparaging the washcloth grip, which had throttled around in his palm causing blisters. For spite, he had torn off the terrycloth, which had ruined the leather underneath, and done damage to the look.

After that, like the tennis racquet companies, Barry and I were at war—Barry with his clunky and cracked Kramer—and I with the sleek wooden Snau, Vitas' racket. I had just entered 9th grade. High school varsity tennis was pretty competitive—although in order to be spring competitive, one had to play winter ball. A great many tennis centers had sprung up for just that reason.

That winter, Tuesdays after school, I practiced with Barry at Windwood Courts. Windwood was cut rate—low budget. The courts had been constructed in an abandoned warehouse—but the cost was right: ten bucks an hour. It was hard to work up a sweat in Windwood. The air hung on you, and by the time your legs un-stiffened, there just wasn't time to get warm. It wasn't worth changing in the basement locker rooms, either, which were freezing. So, like everyone else, I wore my tennis clothes, sweats, and jacket right onto the courts. I didn't like the green carpet either. It was slick and matted. Speed mattered on these courts—speed and reflexes.

Barry was a plugger: a solid straight-A type, who, when compelled to pick a sport, picked tennis. I had to hand it to him though. When Barry put his mind to something, he immersed himself in it completely. The method he had applied with great success to his schoolwork, his dogged grinding, he applied to his game.

Barry came right at you, and he never gave away a point: he never double-faulted; he never hit the ball into the net; and, he rarely hit wide or deep. If he got his racquet on it, one could be assured the ball was coming back loopy and without pace. He made you think you had the goods on him, and then he flipped a lob two or three feet from the baseline. His approaches were so calculated that he rarely lost any points at the net.

The energy of thinking so much, of keeping one's mind perpetually present when playing him was exhausting. More discouraging, Barry's game had no heft. It was more than sufficient, and he won a great deal, but his game was workmanlike. Try as he might, he could never find its heart.

My 14-year mind didn't possess the patience to stay with him though, and my game usually fell apart right before a close of the second set. And after each successive win that winter, even with his cracked racquet, Barry became more confident—an ice-prince, so calculating and clever that he believed he couldn't lose.

After an inevitable second set loss, tennis with Barry dissolved into "Battleball"—a game in which we took opposite sides, five feet from the net and tried to peg each other. The tennis balls came rapid fire, and you used your racquet to block the ball. The only way in or out was to hit or be hit. Simple. If the rock-hard balls didn't hit you, they ricocheted off one of the back walls and rattled around under your feet.

Battleball was great fun—especially when those new pressure-less tennis balls that came in a box were absorbed into your skin, causing a compressed bruise that started small—was barely noticeable—but hurt like hell and overnight intensified and spread out like a blue rash. By the end of each week, Barry and I sported black welts all over our bodies. Mostly they hid beneath our shirts, but every so often, the tentacles of one crept out under our shirt sleeves, a tattoo and testament to our hatred of each other.

When Mrs. Steinmetz, our History teacher, reported Barry's bruises to Mr. Keefer, in Guidance, the world of Battleball collapsed around us. Mr. Keefer interviewed Barry, who said that while under the tennis lights, he had been attacked by gypsy moths that had surged down and sent him running into the fence. Then, Keefer interviewed me, and I said I had been caught in the grips of a malfunctioning ball machine, whose stealth-like ways fired the rock-soggy balls at will and without regard. Had it not been for the sanctity of Battleball, these fabrications would have bolstered our spirits but, we had the good sense to refrain from snickering.

Mr. Keefer sensed that he was over-matched and said flat-out that he didn't have the time, nor the wherewithal, for games. This was a serious matter, he said and assured us the perpetrators would be held accountable.

We had a scare for a while and tried unsuccessfully (after I lost set two) to play doubles with the Windwood croakers, but by the middle of the first set, instead of hitting the ball back over the net, we would hit a kill shot at one another without regard for keeping the ball within the confines of the court. Still, the bruises, various shades of blue, purple, faded to green before they dissolved completely. And, as soon as the bruises faded, all of the hubbub and concern around Barry and me faded, too.

The last time I played Barry was on a particularly wintry day. The roads were crazy-covered and finding our way to Windwood was a challenge. We followed an old Toyota up the steep hill to the indoor courts, and I think without this tether we might not have made it at all.

Windwood's inside was hollow, and except for one other couple hitting the ball back and forth, it was empty. And, because of this, I'm certain, my Snau sprang to life—each serve sounded like a cannon blast and Barry, gun-shy, could barely get his Kramer on most of my serves. Likewise, my returns were like Vitas'. Suddenly I was the playboy: cool, in control, waiting for the Rolls to take me home.

Barry's lobs seemed weighted down by the weather and hung in the air too long, drafted too low to keep my overheads at bay. I reveled as he ran from one side of the court to the other, trying to smack the ball away as if he wanted no part of it. And the balls all bounced in my favor, "lets" dribbled over the net cord on important points, dropping to the carpet with barely a bounce. Match-point kicked off the top of the net and bounced over Barry's leaping overhead attempt. Barry begged for a third set, but I'm sad to say that our 20 bucks had run out.

In the car on the way home, we didn't speak. I kicked-up the am radio and hummed along to the static. Barry kept silent, stewing, pretending to be unflappable but his veneer was visibly cracking.

In the spring, right before I tried out for varsity, I saw an exhibition match between Mac and Vitas in the Civic Arena— an igloo-like dome that was somehow transformed into a tennis court so very similar to the court I played on during the winter. During the match, Vitas was magnificent, hitting the ball from all angles and scooping it up from the carpet, even beating Mac to the net. What struck me and has stayed with me since was the change-over when Mac and alternately Vitas took off their shirts. Each was so thin, he was positively skeletal. And, these were the bad boys of tennis? Bad boys who had taken off their armor and given us a glimpse of their soft underbellies.

After the match, as Barry and I were leaving the Arena, we watched as Vitas made his way through the city in tennis shorts with his Snau leading the way, his legs perfect scissors, his eyes singular and focused, as if making it downtown was all that should matter in the world. This was my one chance to say hello, and I imagined had I not been 14, Vitas would have seen a mirror of himself (I was wearing tennis shorts, too) and taken me clubbing. I hesitated and Vitas Gerulaitis slipped into the night.

GENERATIVE /
ITERATIVE / EVALUATIVE

These are the last days and unfinished pages of a dissertation on *Pragmatics and Features of Sex*, 1998—Beth says—expected by her committee members in two weeks, or at-most, a month. Her defense is in three weeks, but she doesn't think she'll finish. She says she'd happily quit and work in a bank or in a mall selling perfume behind shiny counters—spritzing the stuff on eligible men who will buy it from her with hopes of getting laid. She says even if she quits, she will continue her work, untethered and uncriticized and make her own study of the language of love, its features through natural conversations, speech acts, implicatures, while managing the flow of reference and the theories of the mind. Then, Beth pauses. But it's still too big, she says. It's always too big.

Lance tells her that she "owes it to herself to finish" —comforts her—the first three chapters, generative; convinces her—the second two, iterative; contends—the last, evaluative. "This, after all," he decries, "is defensive writing."

Two weeks prior, Lance, unable to generate a love life, finds himself at the YWCA speed dating: eight minutes per person, then move on. There are the rules. There are always rules.

He meets Beth, a female graduate student—studying cognitive theories of metaphor—Beth—who sits down at the table across from him and tells him within the first minute that when she made plans to reformat her wedding schema, she suddenly found herself single— again. She tells him within the first two that she is lamenting her Overview date. She tells him after three that she has taken to printing multiple drafts of her dissertation chapters and stashing them all around her house, all around her parents' house, all around her pug Beefo's house. She tells him that even after the break-up, there are still multiple copies at her ex-finance's house. At four minutes, she admits she has been having dissertation destruction nightmares: "bad dreams about fires and floods," she says, "bad dreams about the mighty cloud and evaporating pages; bad dreams about unspeakable acts of God"— "All these bad dreams," she says, "conspire against the act of completion." She pauses briefly for effect. She has practiced this.

"Writing so many drafts has been a nightmare," she says, "but," she says she "tries not to take herself or *it* too seriously and *that*," she says, "is precisely the reason why I am speed dating at the YWCA, instead of working on it;" although she admits that she, even now, while talking to Lance, that's his name right? is still thinking about it. She says she is always thinking about it. "What else is there to think about?" she asks and adds as a sad afterthought she, "doesn't remember any more." At six minutes, she asks if she can be so bold and asks Lance if she may leave a copy of it—the dissertation on *Pragmatics and the Features of Sex* framed by theories of tension, controversion, and grammatic deviance and informed by philosophy of metaphor and meaning with him; but, she enumerates, she will only relinquish the pages under the following conditions: 1) that he will, under no condition, read it— 2) that he will put it in his ice box and under no condition, move it, touch it, or let anyone else read it or touch it; 3) that, if they *were* to stop speaking, and he were to read it that, even so, he won't even think about editing it, even for good semantical reasons. With 30 seconds to go, she places an official looking contract spelling out these conditions in front of Lance and asks him to initial it. After he does, she says at speed dating's conclusion, she will provide her contact information on the summative evaluative survey value sheets. Then she moves on.

The next evening, Beth brings her dissertation draft over to his apartment. It is cold to the touch. She talks fast, says she likes speed dating because most of the men she meets are nice and, like Lance, allow her to keep her baby safe with them. She oversees Lance as he places her dissertation, along with the signed contract, in his pretty-empty freezer. Calmer after having watched him scrape out a space and after having deposited it and the contract in the icebox, Beth sits down on his plaid couch and drinks wine straight out of the bottle.

After the first gulp, Beth says she can read Lance. After the second, Beth says she would very much like to write Lance. After the third, Beth points to Ping—Lance's pygmy hedgehog—and makes an off-color remark about having, as a girl, fed apples to a big fat hedgehog who lived near her grandmother's fig tree and swallowed apples whole.

The sex is iterative, then recursive, then iterative. After-talk is sentence-level defensive. There is little attention given to overall meaning. No judgement, Beth says, no evaluation.

Later, Beth pulls on her pants, carefully picks up Ping from his revolving wheel, wraps him in her sweater, says "Insurance" and bolts out the door.

Lance can't say he doesn't learn something about Beth and pragmatics and the features of sex from reading her dissertation: after he finishes reading it, he puts the cold pages under the cushions of his couch, sits on them, pours himself a glass of wine, and stares into Ping's empty cage.

THE TWISTED S

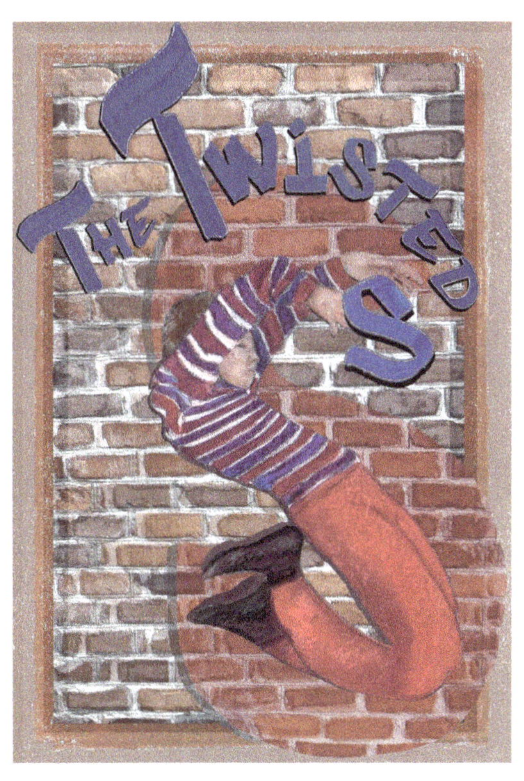

As a child, "the Twisted S," for that's what the other kids called Greg King, Jr., mostly in uninspired uniformity, could literally bend his thin and elastic frame and transform it into the letter S or its inverse, the # 2, although this took a little more doing.

The Twisted S's renown stretched across three overlapping communities, and his shadow was drawn in a chalk-like double-helix over three elementary playgrounds.

His gift was accompanied by a fair degree of athletic acumen, but it was the Twisted S's exploits, detailed by Montel "The Marvel" Bishop, on various fields, in stadiums, in rinks, on turf, grass, wood and clay that ensured S's reputation and promoted and propelled his slippery self into heroic status.

During each game, S's body found itself in nearly every conceivable position more-or-less at the same time and all at once. And each of his impossibly mythic moves was chronicled by the Marvel, who, if he did not have a real microphone, used his fist, the stump of his knee, or one of the Lunch Pail Gang's errant elbows.

Here's the Marvel engaged in a spontaneous moment of superlative broadcast, "Hey sports aficionados: on the football field, the Twisted S finds himself in the shape a coat hanger, his wire hand pulling would-be runners and receivers completely out of their shoes, which try to run on their own toward goal posts but inevitably settle upturned, unnoticed, and knotted on the opposing team's chalky sidelines; on baseball infields, the Twisted S's torso rubber bands while his feet remain grounded, as he stretches from second to third plucking line drives out of the air or snagging choppers from the dirt and tossing them to first so quickly that the rubber band core of the ball arrives long before its soft unfilled cover; on the hardwood, the Twisted S curves more than jumps, blocking and rebounding at will, making hook shots so effortlessly that it looks as if he is dropping them through a kiddie hoop two feet from the floor."

The Marvel, also, made S heroic under his particularly hyperbolic pen that spouted speculatives in the Summervale Elementary's *Daily-Daily*: "There are as many different metaphors as there are games kids can concoct; yet, the Twisted S feels it his natural duty and God-given right to win with resounding authority all of the games he plays. And 'S' does indeed win in the present and will again win in the future, every game, every sport, every pastime into which he twists his flap-sickle self."

There was talk, always in hushed tones, on the playground, by the Lunch Pail Gang, in theory-driven classrooms—serious talk, inserted between lunch trays, of "a boycott, a ban, a believe-it-or-not banishment" from those who put too much stock in parity.

The chief culprit of such disgraceful ruinations was, in fact, also the Marvel himself, a dyed-in-the-wool journalist, who was bad at sports but who, even at the age of 10, had learned the art of the build-up so he could then delight in tearing idols asunder.

At a time in American history when fourth grade boys came to believe they could indeed say whatever it was they wanted because they would one day rule the world, the Marvel verily shouted, at least once a week, usually after he had flubbed an easy play: "Off with his hands, his feet, his arms, his legs, off-off-off with all parts of Greg King, Jr.'s, duplicitous torso; indeed off with the very head of the Twisted S!"

Because this outburst was rendered in the middle of a lesson calling forth antonyms, the Marvel himself was banished to Dr. Spinach's Fibber McGee closet, where he was commanded to stand behind the closed door "quietly and respectfully"—amongst cardboard, crepe paper and glue.

After the better part of an hour, Montel Bishop emerged, flushed face and hair swiveled, as if he'd just struck out in kickball again and had to endure a swirly in Lav #7.

Later during cold cuts and milk, the Marvel, our resident bard, was back in heightened form and figuratively spilled the beans and told the wide-eyed, inflexible and unimaginative Lunch Pail Gang, who sat on the green foldable lunch tables—about how in the darkly-dark, after his perceptive eyes had quite thoroughly adjusted to Fibber McGee, he had found, tucked "way-way-way back behind the crepe paper and glue, stashed between boxes of books and wedged between a discarded bulletin board and a plastic penguin, a *magazine* filled with mens and womens."

The Marvel pronounced "mens and womens" with such solemnity that there was absolutely no doubt that, true or untrue, he meant exactly what he said.

On the playground, later, the Marvel said: "Mens and womens," he quoth, "whose twisted silhouettes were intertwined and all mixed up, bent as if blendered, bodies trying to climb inside each other but that hadn't quite found the right-proper way to do so." Then, with a mischievous grin, he squared around to face Greg King, Jr., and said plainly for all to hear, "And I most assuredly saw the faces of your Momma and Daddy twisted, tempered, and imprinted, unspeakable amongst those torn and ruffled pages."

Indeed, this sudden twist in the Marvel's story was most unexpected—his tales frequently turned fantastical, but not cruel; however, the Marvel had found a way to couch fightin' words within the magazine pages he himself had invented.

Greg King, Jr.'s, own father, "the King," who the Twisted S suddenly saw in his mind's eye, had lectured S many times about the demerits of fighting. And Greg well-understood that if the Twisted S was to succumb to the Marvel's taunts, he would most assuredly find himself, win or lose (and he *never* lost), first in the diabolical clutches of Dr. Spinach, who would undoubtedly pass him like a hairball into the calloused clutches of Mr. Bridge—two tons of vice-principal with absolutely no sense of humor—and, then finally into the steely clutches of his father, Gregory King, Sr., who, after making little Greg write an extended letter of apology to Montel, Dr. Spinach, and Mr. Bridge and following his missives would find all kinds of yard work, gutter cleaning, garage and basement floor scrubbing for him to do.

And, only after Greg King, Jr., had performed all of these tasks to the utmost satisfaction of "the King," he might, and this was highly doubtful, with a prayer and an unlikely miracle, escape the embarrassment of being forced to cut a tree switch that Sr. would shake and wield —its singing wood slicking through the air unable to find its target.

The Marvel's words echoed again on the snow-covered playground: "And I most assuredly saw the faces of your Momma and Daddy twisted, tempered, and imprinted, unspeakable amongst those torn and ruffled pages."

S stood there, legs together, crossed at the ankles, his torso—a wound spring—ready to uncoil and scatter the Marvel's malevolent words, splitting them at first, then shredding them, and finally demulsifying them in front of the Lunch Pail Gang until the Marvel's language vaporized to the far side of declension.

As the Twisted S's spring began to uncoil, it was all he could do to force himself to stop, to hold off—to not obliterate the Marvel completely.

And, in this momentary hesitation of "not-quite-forgiveness"—the Lunch Pail Gang found in S's heart: compassion? For although their inner demons called out for complete obliteration, some part of them would not abide it.

Such disparity between destruction and deliverance happened more-or-less at the same moment, invectives spilled forth from their blood-thirsty tongues—urging the Twisted S to spiral forth uncharacteristically and punch the Marvel in the mouth.

The Lunch Pail Gang full-well knew the conse-quences as they quietly considered departing the scene and would, in not-too-distant-a future, through time and hyperbole, build less substantial myths filled with what happened afterward when fictions are left to run away with themselves.

The Twisted S realized almost immediately after he had thoroughly vanquished Montel "the Marvel" Bishop's words that something about what he had done was almost too American and yet not American at all. And worse yet, the Twisted S, had, in full view of the fourth-grade girls, added insult to injury by uprooting all that was left of the Marvel's vocabulary by dropping bits of his words across the playground for everyone to study like a frog dissected in science class.

Each word from Montel's lips had been desiccated and with even the best dictionary, there was absolutely no way to reconstruct them, not even using the primal code derived from his writings in the *Daily-Daily*—and his poor face, after such a twisted punch, wouldn't, couldn't, be reconstituted.

When the Twisted S unwound completely and surveyed the damage his singular wallop had caused, he was, according to Dr. Spinach— "Dissociative and dispassionate." Mr. Bridge, who could, with the click of a tongue, slow down any cow tipping, used other words, two in fact: "Unremorseful and unrepentant." And even Principal Brown—a bespeckled non-descript rarely-seen-man said that he was concerned that "Greg King, Jr., seemed unfazed and unflustered."

The guidance counselor, Mrs. N, who it was rumored did not believe in God and viewed all things through detached bifocals that scanned lines of 'verifiable data' stacked on her desk in huge unyielding piles, found a way to convey to Greg that, in essence, the Marvel had been, what did she say? "hurt" and that Greg King, Jr., "would have to assume the responsibility."

The exact details were sorted out for the better part of the second half of the day.

Even the head of school security—a stout man named, believe-it-or-not, Francis Drake (aka the Infamous Officer Beef) was summoned to Summervale Elementary's Front Office.

Drake spent most of his time hanging out in the parking lot or composing necessary reports on an old Underwood typewriter closeted in the Security Office—a trailer attached to the elementary school, which was also attached to the Summervale Jr. High.

Having been a former member of a long-ago Lunch Pail Gang himself, Drake met directly with Vice-Principal Bridge, who was interested in determining "precisely what had happened."

Drake moved in and out of Mr. Bridge's office, interviewing everyone who, reportedly, was on the scene. He was unable to obtain a statement from the Marvel, who, because of what was then referred to as a busted lip, was unable to speak a word—"unable to make even the slightest peep."

Then, it started to snow mouthfuls, and the Front Office clogged up like grease, as the basic needs it provided halted. Students stood in unerring lines waiting to be excused; at one point, several members of the jr. high football team rushed in with the appointed task of lifting and carrying sixteen large and prominent boxes filled with football gear that up until then had lined the Office walls like sentries, with the expressed purpose of transporting each box down to the Field House.

Near the end of the day, there were so many students squeezed into the small office area that the football jocks found themselves unable to get through the doors. (And as you might well imagine, they all tried to get through the doors at the same time.)

"The Large One"—Raphael Electric—captain of the defense—tried at first to force his way through the throng but was as quickly forced back and learned that even with an appointed quest to complete, he had better be patient and bide his time.

Summervale Elementary was still running—by itself and on its own accord—but Francis Drake knew this delicate balance could not sustain itself for long—not with the disenfranchised in line and the entirety of the defensive line huddled in the office, not with the busses about to crowd the bus lanes, not with the two-minute warning bell about to chime, and not even with the final tone, which marked a happy counterpoint to a sad afternoon.

Principal Brown waited for some set of official documents or other; the perplexed Mr. Bridge held out his arms and ineffectually said, "Slow down everybody. Just hold your horses;" Coach Caldwell, who had entered the fray wondered what was taking so long and blew his whistle whenever he had the chance: Raphael Electric flexed his muscles, and Dr. Spinach took pictures for the Summervale *Yearly Yearly*.

Snow covered school busses pulled directly behind each other on the curb and many of the bus drivers unfurled the *Daily-Daily*, oblivious to the chaos that Officer Beef feared would "consume the school."

Later quoted, Francis Drake said, "A polyester curtain was descending upon Summervale Elementary, and I had to take off my shoes and bang them on the Front Office counter to gain attention."

The office assistant—Elaine "Wonder Lady" Tendril —looked on in disbelief at Beef when he banged his shoes, and Dr. Spinach was quoted in a mixed metaphor: "The Front Office was a veritable *Lord of the Flies*."

Greg King, Jr., was finally passed into Sr.'s hands as they all sat in Principal Brown's Office, and later, again, in Guidance—waiting for the suspension papers to be officially scanned and sent to the District Office. (Later these self-same papers were strewn akimbo in Sr.'s beater Oldsmobile as father and son waited for each of the full-up snow-drenched busses to finally make a move away from the curb.)

Sr. dutifully followed Francis Drake's poop-brown car, which left the Summervale Elementary School's parking lot and drove for several very long moments.

In their own car—silence—Sr., forcing air in through his nose and out through the mouth; Greg King, Jr., was certain he was on his way to the Youth Home for Delinquent Boys, just this side of Summervale.

It was a cold and gloomy and terrifically snowy day. Everyone on the street, it seemed, was in a terrible mood—freely admitting foul attitudes to anyone who cared to listen. A mountain of snow had found its way to the side of the narrow road and had been manhandled and spilled onto the sidewalks, and this forced the walkers to amble out into the road perambulating against traffic.

It was a wonder that the idiots in the District Office hadn't cancelled school that morning, and damn it if they had, none of this would have happened.

There were five snow days built into the Summervale School schedule, and no one wanted children wandering in the streets along with perturbed traffic.

Yet, wishes are not wants, and there were children running in and around snow banks, weaving in and out of the traffic and fuming cars, packing snowballs and whipping them at each other—and if their errant throws happened to hit a car, they would make their mouths say, "Sorry," to no one in particular.

Seemingly all had returned to normal on this snowy day, which was still not over, which would long be stretched out between the Greg, Jr., and Sr.

Was this the shortest day of the year? The Twisted S knew that it couldn't have been and yet there through the windshield standing in the street in front of them were the remaining members of Lunch Pail Gang, walkers all, who now followed the line of traffic, too, solemnly keeping their heads down.

Had this not happened, the Twisted S would be amongst them—turning and bending himself in S's to avoid the snowballs they half-heartedly heaved in his direction—twisting during the impromptu ice hockey game they spontaneously created, their hard-soled shoes becoming skates, an uneaten apple pie, a puck, and their insteps used to maneuver the pie toward lunch pail goals —the Marvel, the self-appointed announcer should have been there, too, capturing it all for the record—especially the attempt at a goal S would have made, his body shape-shifting into a curved stick by virtue of a Newtonian miracle, and slap-shotting the pie to victory.

Had the Marvel been there as a witness, he might well have narrated it like this: "When, indeed, the Twisted S sees his moment, he bounds rather too fast and falls on the ice, but ladies and esteemed gentleman of Summervale Elementary, all the while he keeps laughing, yes, the Twisted S keeps laughing in the face of the irreconcilable and unrecoverable. And even as a snowplow displaces a snowbank, he remains very prone, immanently stiff, unbending, inelastic, completely rigid, and hereafter a perpetually straight Greg King, Jr., with ambulance siren blaring on the way to Summervale General to be x-rayed."

CLEAN UP IN
THE MEAT DEPT.

I see her in the supermarket. She wears an oversized pink sweatshirt displaying two big cloth cut-out letters that signify sorority. She is maybe thirty, beautiful, and not alone.

Her cart rattles against the unevenness of the shiny supermarket floor. A large man, her boyfriend I imagine, dressed in unmatched wrinkles, stands facing backwards wearing a backward baseball cap on the front of the cart she pushes. I watch as he cleans off various shelves with his broad arm while he uses the heels of his untied sneakers at intervals to slow the cart. "Woody" is written across his massive gray sweatshirt.

"Woody," I murmur to myself.

I maneuver my cart simulating synchronous test-patterns to the cool muzak of "Somewhere (there's a place for us)," grabbing items off the shelves (paper towels, Kool-Aid, caramel brownies, artisan jalapeno bread, baby Swiss cheese, prepared sushi) all the while calculating the purchases in my head, while at the same time positioning myself in front of Sorority, looking backwards more than occasionally.

When I see Woody snap his arm out for a box of animal crackers, I imagine myself having a supermarket affair with his girlfriend.

We would cut coupons using the same scissors and agree to meet in the popsicle aisle until our relationship grew warmer; soon after, she would trust me to squeeze the honeydew melons while she weighed and bagged them; in the veggie aisle, she would scrutinize cucumbers dutifully shrink-wrapped and then, with abandon, run her hands through leafy spinach and broccoli heads looking for bugs; as we grew bolder, together, we would scoop devil chocolate ice-cream into fat funnel cones fresh out of their boxes with no intention of paying; we'd lick our fingers in the good housekeeping aisle and feel dirty afterwards; we'd eye odd-shaped bottles of expensive spicy French mustard and imagine hotdog picnics with our friends drinking out of wine boxes and eating soft buns; we'd push separate carts down the store aisles secretly pleased with our slyness yet recognizing we were under surveillance; we would rub elbows as we clandestinely walked toward Check-Out, and giggle at the blips as our items were scanned by a glittery woman with purple eye makeup and a tiara with a button that read, "I bring the glow;" we'd discover our special award points and Sparkles would call out to the manager, a man with a mustache that curls upward toward the florescent lights, who would take our picture and throw in a Sippy cup advertising the store; then, together we'd hold our bring-your-own bag as we exit, a single orange juice container between us; we'd unlock our separate car doors, my Buick, her Prius, nod to each other, and follow whoever left with the juice.

Ours would not be a brief shopping spree of check-ins and check-outs, receipts and coupons. This girl, who I'd affectionately call Sorority, would know I loved her more than... Corn Flakes, more than corn muffins, more than cornbread with tasty bits of creamed corn, more than corn niblets in cans. Still, no matter how much I'd push, she'd refuse to give up her sweatshirt clad boyfriend.

"What does Woody have that I don't?" I'd ask.

Sorority would cock one eyebrow. Then the other. "Do you really want me to answer that?"

"The only thing I have to fear is frozen food itself. Pleeeeeeeaaaaaasee, take me in out of the cold," I'd beg.

"Don't whine in the wine aisle," she'd say.

In a rare moment of honesty in frozen foods, she'd say, "Okay, you asked for it. I keep Woody around for three reasons."

"I'm prepared for the worst," I'd shiver.

"You owe me double coupons for this."

"I'm prepared to write a paper check and suffer anachronistic condemnation."

"Please know this is against my better judgment... I like Woody because he's funny, he can play golf, and he can dance. I don't expect you to understand."

Sorority's words fade away as I wheel my cart into the present, mirroring her twists, and occasionally looking behind for a turn signal in her eyes. I maneuver my cart with the skill and grace of an ice skater through housewares toward meats.

Out of nowhere, an old lady with a trip ticket sticker on her purse and an out-of-control cart, whose front resembles a cartoon whale face with a child in a front seat holding onto the whale's red nose runs the red-light special and smack dabs into my cart, which flips around sideways displaced in the middle of the meat aisle.

"Shit!" the lady says. "As I've always said, people cannot attend to more than one thing at a time. My grandbaby. Are you alright, little Carl?" she says to the stunned child who looks like he is ready to cry. "I will take a pic of the accident with my phone."

"I'm prone to daydreams," I say.

"It's a good thing this cart didn't swallow you whole," she says, winks, and removes little Carl from the mouth of the whale while holding her phone in her other hand.

Although I am only thirty-five, my mother is always trying to set me up with her blue-haired friends, who, when mom invites me over for bridge, sit inappropriately close and are handsy.

Suddenly Sorority's cart swerves and T-bones the whale, and Woody falls backward in very slow motion into the whale's open mouth.

"My meat," the old lady says to little Carl who immediately begins to cry. "That big man is crushing my meat!"

From inside the whale's mouth, all one can see are Woody's hands holding a big rubber spatula, a box of ant traps, and a beef sirloin. The old lady snaps another picture.

I imagine the headline in Shopper's Guide.

MEAT AISLE MEETING SPOILED BY BOYFRIEND STUCK IN THE MOUTH OF A WHALE

"You weren't looking where you were going and ran into me and Whaley. Thank God, little Carl was not in the cart!" the old lady says to Sorority and snaps another pic.

"Damn right we did!" Woody yells from deep down inside, still waving the spatula.

Sorority blushes. Her eyebrows curl upward. Little Carl continues to cry.

"Today is about being nice, Woody," I say into the mouth of the whale, "let's be trend-setters and upright citizen models for Little Carl."

"Whaley gobbled up that horrible man like plankton," Little Carl yells.

"Who you calling a whale?" Woody yells.

"Somehow I feel the fault is mine," I say to Sorority.

"Asshole!" from the depths.

"Lady ears," the old lady repeats.

"Fuck you!" Woody says.

"Lady ears, lady ears, lady ears," the old lady covers little Carl's.

"My name is Chuck," I extend my hand to Sorority.

"Annie," Sorority says.

"I would have taken you for a Martha or Maddie," I say.

"Glad to know you, Chuck. Fancy meeting you in the meat department," Sorority says.

"Should we exchange coupons or wait for the manager?" I say.

"Oh, let's exchange numbers," the old lady says.

"Listen Pal," Woody's voice comes out of the whales' mouth all echoey. "You better shut it before I stuff something in it!"

"Oh, I get it: like the food chain," I say. "And, you're the itty-bitty fish…" Woody drops the spatula and the ant traps and the meat and tries to get up out of the cart, which rumbles and moves on its own accord precariously close toward the pot roasts all stacked and sealed in plastic.

"Somewhere!" I get on one knee and sing to Sorority. "There's a supermarket for us."

"Oh, I just love that song, Chuck!" The old lady says and takes another picture as Whaley spills over sideways and dumps Woody and its contents onto the floor.

The manager turns the corner and yells, "Clean up in the Meat Dept. Stat!"

"You better run buddy," Woody yells from the cart. "What the hell was that all about, Annie? Do you know that guy?"

"Stick it, Woody."

"Lady ears to you, too, young lady."

I stand in the parking lot with my two bags of groceries and watch a store employee dressed in a white shirt and a bow tie try to run a stack of 30 carts too many toward the front entrance. The first cart in the runaway train chugs fearlessly toward little Carl, unaware, who stands on the ramp in front of the store staring at a red gumball.

I see myself running like the wind, surpassing the carts, and in a single bound and with superhero strength, grinding the runaway train to a halt, derailing grocery carts and saving the child, who miraculously doesn't drop his gumball.

When I open my eyes, Woody is holding the child safely in his bulging arms. The carts are stopped. The cart runner, startled, tie askew, name tag hanging by a thread from his shirt, sits on the ground with his head in his hands. He looks at Woody. He looks at Sorority. He looks at the carts and the old lady and the store manager. He looks at little Carl.

Sorority stands clutching grocery bags to her sorority letters. She kisses Woody full on the mouth and the child on the forehead. They pose while the old lady takes a picture.

I set my bags on top of my Buick, grab the package of paper towels that stick out of the top of the bag, and throw it toward Woody and Sorority and little Carl and the cart runner and the old lady and the manager; the wind catches hold of the package and blows it back way over my head and out into the parking lot behind me.

FLY STAND, INQUIRE HEREIN

This trip, alone, to the mailbox for Elenore, 80, is filled with hope and dread and is the only real exercise she participates in daily. Still, there are all kinds of stumbling blocks: the front door swells, and it takes wrist-breaking effort to even open it. Elenore ignores the front door and uses the back: there are the uneven steps; there are the weeds; there is the large branch that appears to have broken off sometime during the night and now hangs down by its tenuous wooden tendon; there is the choppy-grassy driveway, the measured steps up the steep hill, the cars and trucks rushing by, nearly sweeping her off her feet.

While standing in the middle of Red Coach Road, she uses her cell phone to call Esther and imagines the beam shooting straight up to the satellite and then making its way back down and into her friend and neighbor Esther's phone. Elenore desperately wants Esther to know where she is—that she is undertaking this journey to the mailbox and is right now standing in the middle of the road, alone. Why have a cell phone if you don't answer it? Still Esther is 90 and sometimes doesn't know how to push the buttons and answers her GrandPad on mute. As Elenore makes her way forward over the uneven pavement, she notes that people don't take kindly to being told what is and what isn't appropriate.

A white mini-van rushes past, far too close, and one of its occupants yells, "Old laaady—100 points!" This snaps Elenore back to her purpose, which is to make it up the hill to the mailbox in front of the house in one piece.

The boy, her son, Albert, had been a beautiful child,

wide-eyed, curious—awake at odd hours. Albert had spent most of his time with his imaginary friend V—he described him as a purplish creature who liked Jell-O and playing "Rat Killer Detective" in the run-off drain that ran adjacent to the house. Other than V, Albert had no real friends but was seemingly unaffected by the separation between reality and unreality in that he genuinely understood living was performed in the moment and not in some distant future or murky past. This made him seem old. Whenever Albert saw Elenore, no matter what machinations he was involved in, he would come running, and, if he could, would find ingenious ways to leap into her arms. This was Albert— happy to be where he was.

S ometimes one finds Albert, just-appeared, a full-figured form across the street with a sippy-cup in his right hand walking beside V. Both V and Albert always look both ways before they make it across the street; they stop at the mailbox and each time Albert introduces V to Elenore, the purplish creature smiles with jagged teeth in an upturned mouth, while the boy gathers the mail—good Albert. Then, he deposits the mail in her hands, and Albert and V turn away after waving goodbye. Dear, dear Albert.

.   .   .

Now, Elenore waits at the mailbox for Albert and V to appear. No Albert, though, just V standing on his furry legs, waving at her like some H.R. Pufnstuf.

"Where's Albert?" she yells across the street.

Elenore waits a moment longer, and when V just stands there silently, she repeats rudely, "Where's Albert?"

V's this Muppety creature who had been a part of Albert's imagination, and she had indulged that imagination whenever she could. She had, after all, set up the cups for the tea party, and helped Albert make tea for his special friend. And, Albert had tried to introduce V to her on many occasions. Elenore had done her part as a mother and had looked right through V as if he were there. Albert had been increasingly unsatisfied with her response and had, for a while, requested only purple clothes and purple shoes and purple hats so maybe she could acclimate herself to the wide and various purple prism of colors that composed V.

"To let him know we love him and he is welcome." The irony was not lost on her when Albert confirmed that his favorite color was green, but still, he would only wear purple.

And then, when wearing purple clothes did not produce the desired effect, one day Albert asked his mother for rat poison because the rats in the sewers had made babies and then the babies had made babies and so on until there were so many rats that they could make a movie. Well giving a child rat poison was definitely not in the *Good Mother's Handbook* and Elenore refused and she made sure to call Esther and tell her to refuse, too, even if Albert and V brought her cookies. And this was funny, kind of, if it weren't so serious because Albert found the rat poison anyway and put it in the teacups and he and V invited the rats to the tea party. "They drank and drank and were dead by high noon," Albert said. "I didn't feel good about it, but it had to be done because of the plague that took the kids in the Pied Piper story that I read to the rats out of the picture book. I think they understood but that didn't make death any easier. NO!"

Satiated, the rats all crawled off into the sewer with bloated bellies to die and then in Biblical proportions the flies came to feast on the rats and the feasted flies got as big as quarters and were angry to boot. They swarmed out of the sewer's great mouth and the rat killer detectives had to find a solution to save the neighborhood from the sixty-five diseases they carried including typhoid, cholera, and intestinal myiasis. And there were pinworms, roundworms, and tapeworms. Albert once heard a girl in his fourth-grade class had a tapeworm as long as her arm and she had to be dewormed with apple cider vinegar and pumpkin seeds because her mother didn't believe in medicines. He told Elenore he didn't want that.

Albert was ingenious, really, and out of the fly strip of his imagination created the Fly Stand. He doused himself in her lavender perfume and challenged the sewer and collected the large horse flies that had hatched and hovered about his head like bullets. Elenore had to admit that Albert had a way with the flies. He told Elenore that both he and V spoke in a special buzz saw language and that calmed the flies that he named: Yacht and Aught and Naught, Sought, and Caught. Come to think of it, as Elenore stood there facing V, the creature looked like a fly—purple and green with that weird beard and those popping eyes.

Albert continued to collect the flies, coercing them into purple-colored jars he had uncovered in the basement. When his father was alive, they used to place lighted candles in the purple jars and line them up on Red Coach Road on Christmas Eve. The luminaries gave off an eerie purple light and were supposed to guide the Christ Child to people's homes.

Albert used a rusty awl he also found in the basement to punch holes in the lids of the jars. He informed Elenore that he planned to sell the flies in jars like other unimaginative kids sold lemonade. He set up the card table that Elenore sometimes used for bridge in front of Red Coach Road beside the mailbox, and he made a sign "Fly Stand, Inquire Herein."

Elenore had no intention of stifling the boy's creativity, but this was too much. Besides, it was gross and unhealthy in both sanitary and psychological terms.

First, V; then, Rat Sewer Detectives, then the rats, then the poison, then the flies and now this—A Fly Stand: the selling of jars of flies, right on the street and right outside the house.

What was even more disturbing was that people actually stopped their cars and "inquired" and often left with a jar of flies. What the heck?

Cars of all types would pull off the road, all aslant and cock-eyed. The traffic would back up; impatient suburban drivers would press their horns; money would change hands; and the people who bought the jars of flies marveled at their size and took away the purple tinged jars to wherever one might put such things.

Elenore heard later that some people took the jars to special places like cemeteries and opened them and let the flies go in search of their loved ones; others left the fly jars in neighbors' mailboxes—neighbors who had been ugly to them at one time or another. One boy, Elenore heard, made a living fly collection—stuck each of the creatures with pins to a Styrofoam board and presented the collection to a teacher he positively hated and watched with mirth as the teacher gasped in horror as she watched the flies all moving clockwise around on the pins. Elenore heard that one girl unleashed the files in her nemesis' locker at school and waited in delight until it was opened and yelled gleefully, "I don't have a problem with anger. I have a problem with you."

And, all the while, there was the empty chair that sat beside Albert, presumably for V, who Albert told her tended to the Fly Stand and spoke their special language and calmed down Yacht and Aught and Naught, Sought, and Caught when they changed hands, but said nothing.

Elenore hated to admit it, but she even broke down and bought a jar of flies herself. Even now, she couldn't believe she had done it. She tentatively handed over the dollar to Albert, who treated her purchase like every other transaction and deposited it with his thin fingers into the purple purse he had asked her to buy from the Sun Drug to "keep the money safe."

Elenore found in herself the opposite of expectations after she bought the jar. Instead of being repelled by it as she had expected, she became fascinated with the swirling movements within the jar and the faint electric buzz sound within, as if each insect called out to be noticed. She placed the jar on the kitchen wood slab table, where she positioned keepsakes and other jars filled with water and assorted plants. The buzz kept her company for a while and then, without her remembering it, became faint and died away.

Albert had a "Fly Counting Contest." He placed a large glass pickle-jug on the card table and for ten dollars one could attempt a guess at the number of flies that swirled around in it. Each contestant would write his or her name and guess on a slip of paper and hand over the ten. Albert promised the entrants half of the winnings. He had already collected $250. And, all the while, Elenore imagined that V sat there smiling, never saying anything, keeping the flies calm and comfortable. Elenore wondered if the other customers could see V. And then she thought that maybe V wasn't an imaginary friend after all but represented some evil force the universe had not yet come to terms with.

The whole enterprise was so very odd and terrifying and troubling and terrible and was happening right in front of her eyes. But what was she to do? The boy was making money, wasn't he? And she believed greatly in creativity and the imagination and responsibility and couldn't conceive that Albert was like those artists who immersed crucifixes in urine or pinned themselves to canvases, leaving parts of themselves there. No! Albert was a dear, sweet boy, who had been led astray. Her dear, sweet boy under the spell of his imagination or its facsimile that sat right beside him, she imagined, holding out the purple jars in his furry paws. Elenore thought that if she could just find a way to convince Albert to give up the Fly Stand and return all of the contest money before something terrible happened, everything would be a-okay and return to semi-normal. But, Elenore could feel something terrible was on the way; she just knew it.

Now Elenore was standing in front of V. She wanted to ask V if it had seen the car coming. What was he thinking as it zoomed out of control up the hill, its front bumper pointing at the Fly Stand? Had Albert said anything to him?

Maybe V was not even standing there; maybe it was her imagination, and the neighbors were watching out their front windows as she talked to the air. The world was like that—a strange and unimaginable place.

But here was the truly strange thing—the unexpected thing that made life worth carrying on. V, whose furry right hand was behind his back, proffered her a purple jar instead of the mail and Elenore took it up without thinking as one would a handshake. And inside were not the buzzy flies that she expected but a lit candle.

V offered the jar to her and she nodded and wanted to ask questions. What were Albert's last words? Did V miss Albert as much as she did? Was Albert happy where he was? Where was he now? Why wasn't he here? Had something happened to him? She expected V to emit some strange buzzing language that she wouldn't be able to understand. She expected V had some answers, some solution. Maybe she would see Albert tomorrow, and she would ask him herself.

The creature watched her as she made her way back down Red Coach Road, her tentative footsteps finding their way across the driveway that was half covered in grass, up the back steps, sidestepping the branch that lay like a misplaced modifier in her backyard and in through the back door, safely into the confines of her house.

Elenore, V noted, never once thought about how she had forgotten the mail but was far more concerned about making sure the flame inside the purple jar remained lit.

SEPTEMBER 29, 1972

S ante hated funerals. Sante's best friend, Bobby Whinny, hated them, too. Bobby said funerals "stole his happiness," and he was filled with such "little happiness" that he hated when what little he had was stolen.

Sante admired Bobby because he made a great deal about not caring about what other people thought. Bobby even went so far as to say he didn't have any feelings. He was like that.

Sante's father, who cut the grass with religiosity and suffered the terrible arthritis, told Sante, "Never trust that Bobby Whinny."

Sante's father said that he couldn't quite put his finger on it, but he believed Bobby was an instigator and that instigators never themselves got in trouble. "They pick at a scab, Sante, until you can no longer stand it and then you rip it off yourself and bleed. It leaves a scar, son, and when you look at it over the years, you remember how that scar came to be. Stay a safe distance from Bobby Whinny," his father said, "if there is ever enough distance one would consider safe. Personally, I doubt it."

Now, Bobby Whinny's own father was dead, and Sante and everyone at school and all of the fathers and mothers and teachers were expected to show up for the viewing on Friday. Some of the parents, Sante heard, thought twelve-year-olds were too young to see death up-close. Mann Middle School's Math teacher, Mr. Cave, said, "You all need to be respectful at the viewing; observe it silently: that is why you have two ears and two eyes and only one mouth and one tongue. You're all smart enough to know this. I shouldn't have to do the math."

The only other dead person Sante knew had been his grandfather, his namesake, who had dropped dead on the railroad tracks he'd patrolled.

Sante imagined a noble death for his namesake: maybe he'd taken a bullet between the eyes or had been cracked on the skull with his own flashlight by train robbers who had wrestled it away from him.

Old Sante's casket had been closed.

Sante suspected that the death of Bobby Whinny's father marked one of those moments old people talked about constantly—one of those moments when you tried to hold the world in your hands but it kept shifting and changing, no matter how much you wanted to slow it down.

Bobby Whinny's father had always been something of a shadow. Sante only met him once, one week prior to his death, and this was only because Bobby had won tickets to see a Pittsburgh Pirates' baseball game on September 29, 1972, having been the thirteenth caller to 13Q—the local radio station they listened to with religiosity.

Bobby had bragged and bragged about having won the tickets, and Sante was surprised when Mr. Whinny called his father and asked if he would "allow Sante to come with them to the outing." That's what Mr. Whinny had called it—like it was a picnic or something.

At first, Sante's father said "No" straight out. It was only after Sante begged a billion-gazillion times that his father relented, and Sante suspected this was only because Roberto Clemente, Sante's father's hero, was poised to join ten other players in the 3000 Hit Club.

Even so, Sante's father said, "Don't trust that Bobbie Whinny any farther than you can throw him, and I suspect the baseball doesn't usually fall too far from the tree."

Friday evening, September 29, 1972, regular season game 149, was the first of three games with the Mets— the finale series of the season.

Mr. Whinny picked Sante up at 6:30 pm sharp in a red Mustang that glistened in the setting sun. Bobby wore a white Pirate's jersey, a yellow P-cap, and his glove, whose pocket expanded just-so when he caught a ball; he had the stub of a pencil behind his ear to mark-up the program his father would surely buy him.

Sante, on the other hand, wore a stained knock-off t-shirt, a dirty black P-cap with a bent bill, and carried his ratty glove under his armpit. He felt terrifically embarrassed when his father handed him a quarter right in front of everybody and told him to use a pay phone at Three Rivers Stadium to "check-in" during the seventh-inning stretch.

Mr. Whinny wore a three-piece suit, a vest, a blue tie and what Sante knew to be a cravat. Bobby didn't say a word about the suit or the vest or the tie or the scarf, but during the drive to Three Rivers Stadium, he kept rolling his eyes, making crazy circles with his fingers, and clandestinely pointing to his father, who drove on unaware.

They all sat way up in the orange seats in the right field section of the third deck of Three Rivers and watched the stadium below fill with white jerseys and yellow caps.

This was the best 13Q could do?

Before the game started, Mr. Whinny bought three hot dogs, three cotton candy's, three Cracker Jacks and three Cokes.

From the very first moment they took their seats, Bobby Whinny yelled until he became terrifically hoarse. Sante matched yells for a while until the tendons of his jaw ached and then got tired of yelling and settled down into his seat and awaited the first pitch from Nellie Briles to Met's Wayne Garrett, who promptly singled to right. But, in a moment of redemption, Ken Boswell, the Met's second baseman, grounded to Willie Stargell at first, who turned it to Jackie Hernandez at short, who stepped on second and fired it back to Stargell for a double play.

The entire stadium found its voice along with Bobby and went crazy.

Then, aging Tommy Agee, who was leading the Mets in RBI's despite a 227 average, grounded to Hernadez, who threw for the second time to Stargell to end the top of the first.

Bobby yelled, "Way to go, Willie," who ran off the field toward the dugout.

The bottom of the first, Clemente, batting third, was going for his 3000th hit.

The night was warm, and suddenly the stadium lights popped on—a million eyes, a million shining suns. For an instant, the field was whitewashed with the lights competing for survival with the day's dying light. Then, eyes adjusted and a field of possibilities spread out before them.

Future Hall of Famer Tom Seaver was pitching.

All season, Seaver led the Mets in pitching categories, but during his warm-ups, he looked unsteady in a nervous kind of way.

First up, right-fielder and utility player Vic Devallio promptly walked. That sparked the crowd.

Bobby sat up straight in his seat, pounding his hand in his glove. Dave Cash, Pittsburgh's wiry second baseman, who picked up every hop and skip at second like he was collecting jellybeans, took a few from Seaver, and then disappointingly flew out to right.

"And now Roberto Clementeeeee!!!" the announcer yelled as the stadium organ piled up notes in crescendo.

All stood in anticipation as Clemente took the plate. Willie Stargell, clean-up batter, with feet solidly planted in the on-deck circle, wind-milled his thick bat, as if willing Roberto home.

Baseball found both pause and poetry and then set them in motion: each moment a possibility.

Seaver: Tom Terrific, The Franchise, Future Hall of Famer, three-time Sy Young Award winner, twelve All-Star appearances, no size, no strength, unbelievable control.

Clemente: who could throw a ball in a straight line from the warning track home; whose legs moved so quickly he could run extra bases with barely a bobble by a fielder; who felt he had been robbed and overlooked for eighteen seasons; who felt as if he had more than earned every run, every walk, every hit, every ball. Roberto, their hero—the humble humanitarian, selfless to a fault, uniform always pressed and form surprisingly thin from great heights; whose bat spoke for him. No one could deny this moment was about him.

That delicious pause and then Seaver delivered the pitch, which came off the bat with a snap. Seaver jumped but the ball sailed just beyond his glove and hit the dirt and took a quick hop. Boswell, the second baseman, charged, bobbled the ball and, as the paper later said, "Threw to first in an attempt to get the streaking Roberto." The paper said, "A large number thought there was no way Boswell could have thrown out Clemente who was over the bag several seconds before the baseball got there."

"It's a hit," Bobby yelled. "3000 for sure!"

"It's an error," Mr. Whiney said.

"It's a hit, Dad."

"Face facts, Bobby. You live way too high in the clouds."

"Why else would they be waiting so long to post it?"

"That's why they are waiting because it's an error, but they want to make sure they get their ducks in a row because, no matter what, they'll have some explaining to do."

Then, the umpire shook his head. And there it was—a big E on the scoreboard followed by the diminishing chords of the stadium organ and the scattered boos, and then, like that, everyone collectively let out a breath and took their seats.

Roberto said later, "They have done this to me all the time. Just because I speak my mind and tell them what I think they give me the shaft and take many hits away from me... There was no question in mind about it being a hit. But this is nothing new. Official scorers have been robbing me of hits like this for eighteen years."

"He was robbed," Bobby said and looked up from the program he was scribbling in.

"Get over it," Mr. Whinny cautioned.

"Fucking-A robbed."

"Watch your tongue, Robert!"

"It's like you're more happy you're right than..."

"That's life, Bobby—a series of errors—and I somehow doubt you'll learn from your mistakes."

"But it was a mistake, Dad. A mistake by the scorer."

"Face facts. The game is bigger than one player, Bobby. And, it's certainly bigger than your opinion."

And, as if on cue, the crowd around them let out its breath and sat on their hands.

Bobby marked an "E" in the program.

Even through clean-up batter Willie Stargell was up

with his great round-house swing and his own star power, it didn't seem to matter anymore.

And then it all went to hell. Clemente went down swinging in the fourth and flummoxed in the sixth by Dave Cash's attempted steal at second, he half-heartedly dribbled one to first for an easy out.

Aside from the quick phone call Sante made during the seventh inning stretch, the world had collapsed.

Bobby and Sante and Mr. Whinny were all bunched up like three kings sitting in orange thrones; in Sante's mind, they had become baseball brothers, who would take a bean-ball for each other; sacrifice whatever, whenever, lay down a bunt, even if they had a chance at hit 3000. The stadium lights were a thousand shining benevolent eyes as the visible world, it seemed, had been waiting for Roberto Clemente's last at-bat, and every boy and perhaps every man's secret fantasy was to be #21, one pitch away from his 3000th hit—"And you can kiss it goodbye!"

There would be no homerun catch—they were too high up and in foul ball territory for that. Still, Sante put on his ratty glove that he had worn during the first four innings until his hand became too hot, and he had stashed the glove under the seat.

Mr. Whinny even loosened his cravat and had taken off his suit coat by the time Clemente came up to the plate. Seaver was working on a two-hitter, but the stadium crowd wasn't paying much mind.

The pitcher and batter looked at each other with begrudging respect. There was a long pause, like before a sneeze, as Seaver waited for the sign and brushed it off. The stadium held its breath, and the pitch came off the bat like applause destined to clear the right field wall for sure. It had the distance but suddenly hooked right toward them.

Sante held up his glove. He could see the ball's seams, which ran across it like a perfectly sewn-up monster, and the ball just kept coming. He waited for the solid leather smack.

At the very last instant, Bobby Whinny pushed Sante out of the way, jumped in front of him, held up his shaky glove, and caught the ball in his expandable pocket. As if forced into his seat by the imaginary ball stuck fast in the pocket of his ratty glove, Sante saw all 24,193 fans on their feet applauding Bobby Whinny, who held the ball aloft toward the thousand shining lights.

Three Rivers Stadium erupted in crazy delight that such a "little boy" had made the grab of a lifetime. Well, maybe not a lifetime, but the catch of the game.

Alas, Roberto Clemente did not get his 3000th hit that Friday night. After the foul ball, he hit a long drive to right field and Rusty Staub pulled it down. Momentum gone, Stargell and Oliver quickly struck out. The Pirates lost 1-0.

Even though it should have been festive, the ride home in the red Mustang was not. Bobby Whinny, the big baby, was sulking because his father refused to take fifty extra minutes and stand outside the Players' Exit to Three Rivers Stadium so Bobby could get Roberto's autograph.

"Only die-hard Pirate fans do that," Mr. Whinny said. "We're amateurs, right, Sante?" Sante didn't dare shake his head either way as Bobby threw dart-eyes in his direction.

Bobby argued that after such an amazing catch, he deserved to be in the Pirates' Locker Room. "To meet Roberto!"

And then Mr. Whinny spoke in a measured tone that chilled Sante. "How do you think you and your friend are able to go to games like this and eat their fill and even have the opportunity to catch foul balls? I'll tell you why because your father has to get up impossibly early and stretch his wet rubbers over his work shoes and put on his red plastic nose and climb into his clown car and go to Fucking Work!"

Sante had never heard an adult drop the F-Bomb on purpose; once his father had almost cut off the tip of his middle finger with the lawn mower blade and came running into the house yelling "Fuck, Fuck, Fuck," but that was somehow very different.

Bobby Whinny said, "Look at me, Dad! I did something special."

"Yes you did, so drop the attitude and get over yourself."

By the time the red Mustang pulled into his driveway, Sante was glad to get out of the car, filled with palpable silence.

Tomorrow was Saturday and the prospects of the weekend loomed large. Sante said his goodbyes, shook Mr. Whinny's hand, thanked him more times than he knew he should have, and made his way up the crooked back steps and in through the back door, holding his glove—the unmoving headlights of the car illuminating his way with a silent stare.

Sante brushed his teeth, buttoned his PJs, pulled the race car bedspread down and climbed into bed before he uncovered the bulge in his ratty glove and found the pocket filled to its limit with the ball. The ball that Roberto had hit—the ball from that night. Bobby Whinny's ball.

Saturday, Sante and his father listened to the radio and the strikeouts continued with Clemente whiffing in the first inning.

Finally, in the bottom of the fourth, first up, he did it! —a lined-double to left center against the pitcher, Matlac.

Sante and his father ran around the living room holding couch cushions and bouncing off one another.

"Hold on tight!" They had just seen history.

And then, with Stargell up, a passed ball made it by Met's catcher Schneck and Clemente stole third standing up. And the announcer on the radio said, "Clemente not only got 3000 but might score, too."

Richie Zisk walked. Now the players were on first and third. Clemente watched his friend, catcher Manny Sanguillén, approach the plate.

Clemente and Sanguillén seemed to have some undisclosed understanding, a way of communicating with their eyes.

"Manny, oh, Manny," Sante prayed.

"And Sanguillén singles to left and Clemente scores!

Clemente scores! And wait, hold on tight, it's not over Pirate fans."

"It's not over Pirate fans!" Sante and his father both yelled at the radio!

"HOLD ON TIGHT!" his father yelled.

"A right," Sante yelled.

"Jackie Hernandez hits a triple. He hits a triple, and Zisk scores easily and here comes Manny with his crazy-churning windmill legs, he rounds third, as if on a string and meets his best friend at home! What an inning, Pirate fans. What an inning!"

"What an inning!" Sante yelled at his father.

"Hold on, tight!"

It was odd, though, because when the time came for Clemente's final at bat, Bill Mazeroski was sent in to pinch hit for him. It made no sense, but no one was going to complain about "Maz," who was the hero of the 1960 World Series and hit a homerun against the Yankees in the bottom of the ninth. The Pirates won the second game of the series 5-0.

And, after the game, Willie Mays left the dug-out and shook hands with Roberto.

"I felt kind of bashful when the fans cheered," Clemente said, "I'm a very quiet, shy person although you writers might not believe it because I shout sometimes."

And none of this mattered because soon after the game, they got a phone call. Bobby Whinny's father was dead, and Sante and all of the others had to attend the viewing at the end of the week.

Monday, Sante visited Bobby at home to listen to the

final game of the series. The Pirates lost 7-3, and Bobby was inconsolable. He kept talking about having caught the ball. He said it all didn't make sense to him that it was gone. "You saw me catch it, right?"

Tuesday, Bobby insisted on returning to school, and during recess, a baseball bounced off his fingertips—actually breaking one of his fingers.

Wednesday, he came to school—even more miserable—with a metal splint on his finger, and he sat on the hillside and watched everyone else play. Injured boys usually fulfilled the role of umpire—an unpleasant and unwinnable task, yet no one dared look in Bobby's direction.

Thursday, Bobby decided to play, even with his broken finger. While swinging at ball four with one arm, the bat slipped out of his hand, broke through a window and landed in the smack-middle of Mr. Cave's classroom.

Friday, almost a week after his father's death, Sante wondered if he should give the ball back to Bobby at the viewing in front of everyone: it seemed like the right thing to do. Perhaps this was a test.

At the very last moment before he and his father were about to leave for the viewing, Sante palmed the ball in one motion and slipped it into the front pocket of his suit jacket. It made a terrible bulge.

His father made Sante turn around for inspection and said, "I've noticed lately you have the tendency to slouch, to keep your hands in your pockets; today is a day you'll need to stand up straight and show support for your friend. This is the way it will need to be from now on."

Sante stood tall in his suit, still holding the ball in his pocket. His father's hands found the car keys and together they made their way downstairs, out the door, and climbed into their trusty Oldsmobile.

At the viewing, Sante waited in a very long line that stretched out the door. He took in the talk and realized that at funerals adults operated under a whole different set of rules: politeness, serious and sequential nods, secret smiles, handshakes, passwords, side-long glances.

The line didn't surge as much as creep. Friends, teachers and parents moved, didn't move, and moved again.

Bobby Whinny stood in a pin-striped suit and golden, thick-knotted tie beside his mother in front of the long casket. His hair was swiped to the side by a brush-back hand. His eyes were set solid, and his hands were silent.

When the consoling parties held out their hands for the customary handshake, Bobby Whinny waited out the uncomfortable pregnant pauses. Instead of dropping their hands in silent disapproval, men and women reached out and tousled Bobby Whinny's hair—said something like, "It'll be okay, son. Just give it time."

The line jerked forward again, and Sante felt that anxious, overpowering feeling of morning alarm clocks and unforgiving, itchy wool clothes. This gave way to watching the second hand on the funeral parlor's wall clock click by, trying to catch the minute hand. And Bobby Whinny looked like someone you should feel sorry for, standing next to the casket in his suit and his wide tie with his splinted finger—a boy tangled up in a string of perpetual bad luck.

Mrs. Whinny talked with Sante's father for a long time; she inquired about his job and asked about the lighter things in life. Then, she bent over at the waist and her very lips touched Sante's ear, "Promise me, Sante, you will watch out for Bobby? You will, won't you?"

Sante shook his head but couldn't even look at Bobby and felt terrible about himself because he realized that he cared more for keeping things the way they were than the way they were supposed to be.

And, then the moment shifted from work talk to the irrevocable sadness of crisp, cold autumn nights and baseball games called short for lack of light.

And there it was.

By the time he swiveled his neck around to look back at Bobby, the procession had already surged forward on its own accord, and Sante was walking beside his father toward the funeral parlor's exit.

Before reaching the door and venturing out into a world where he could no longer look back, Sante broke free of his father and circled toward Bobby, who was contemplating his shoes.

As Sante approached, Mrs. Whinny was in the middle of a conversation with Mr. Cave, who was saying something about time being the great equalizer and divider. He looked down at Sante from his great height— "Sante?"

Sante peered down into the casket that stretched out in front of him—long, metallic, permanent. Mr. Whinny's thrush of white hair was remarkably soft when he touched it. Sante felt disapproving looks from the others and pulled the baseball from his pocket and forced it into Mr. Whinny's hand—whose cold wooden fingers didn't seem to want to accept it at first but then wrapped themselves around the ball with a firm grip, fully covering it.

Roberto Clemente died on New Year's Eve, 1972. His overloaded plane crashed during his humanitarian mission carrying supplies to earthquake victims in Managua. The DC 7 plane crashed at 9:22 pm. The plane took off, banked to the left, and then exploded.

Clemente insisted on making the trip to ensure the supplies got into the proper hands. The Coast Guard circled and found the plane on New Year's Day.

There's a black and white picture in the newspaper of Manny Sanguillén, who didn't attend the funeral but went scuba diving in search of his friend's body. After picking through the underwater wreckage, Manny said, "He said to me, 'You are the only friend I ever had.' For some reason we meshed together so I'll never forget that." Roberto Clemente's body was never found.

The last time Sante saw Bobby Whinny was mid-January. Bobby and his family were moving to Chicago, and Pittsburgh was pulled under by a paralyzing snowstorm. Its streets were impossible to navigate, and snowplows had nowhere to pile the heaps of snow, so they left dirty white mountains beside the roads.

School was closed, and a bitter cold gripped the state. Baseball season was long gone—a distant memory, a spring dream that would most assuredly arrive like their allergies.

Of all things, Sante's father had said on that crazy-snowy day that he had a hankering for ice-cream and not some half-baked store-bought sundae but the real deal. "It will be the closest thing we have to an adventure today," his father said and licked his lips. "I want a banana split with marshmallow drizzled over and strawberries mixed in with the vanilla and maybe pineapple, too. I haven't decided.

Let's crank up the machine."

His father found the ancient ice-cream maker in the basement. The old wooden bucket with a crank-stir that had been his grandfather's—his namesake—and Sante remembered when he was very young, the slow process of mixing the ingredients and then cranking the machine until his arm felt like it was going to fall off into the wooden bucket; but, no complaining was allowed. Just a look from his grandfather's askew and serious eyes under those thick opaque glasses he wore caused Sante to think twice about complaining even once. And, then the ice-cream came out smooth and buttery in chunks, and he never in his life remembered tasting anything as good.

Together, Sante and his father made their way toward a mountainous snowbank in their backyard and were in the midst of putting a handful of snow to clean the wooden bucket when Sante saw Bobby standing up-top Cemetery Hill, adjacent to their backyard.

Cemetery Hill was the highest point in Westview and right behind their house. In winter, kids rode their sleds over the tops of the icy grave-slick markers.

"Profound disrespect," the old people said, but their complaints never amounted to much; Westview Police would trudge up the hill and chase the kids away, but inevitably the kids would return the next day and speed over the tops of the graves in an exhilarating rush that made old people want to scream.

In the fading cloudy light, Sante watched Bobby lift his arm and suddenly there it was in the air, hurling toward them in an arc—a snowball hanging for one perfect second at its apex, selecting its target from a great height.

Then, it came crashing down upon his father, who was so surprised that he almost fell over.

Without a second thought, Sante took off running up the hill. Bobby just stood there as Sante made shorter the distance between them. Sante reached down, packed snow between his thick palms and sent the big fat tight snowball hurling toward Bobby, who, backpedaling, snagged the snowball from the air put it into his coat pocket and dissolved behind a snowbank.

When Sante finally reached the hill's crest, he realized that he had already ruined his shoes, the coat he was wearing, adequate for short trips, was no match for this weather, and that the chase was lost.

Sante motioned with a whirlwind of arms for his father to come up the hill and join him. "It's great up here, Dad" he yelled. "I never really understood how great it is up here."

After the 1972 baseball season ended in October, Bill Mazerosky said he was retiring. Clemente said, "He is the greatest second baseman of all time, a real superstar. But people forget too fast what he has done for the Pirates. Nobody I ever saw could field with him. He won the

World Series in 1960 with his home run against the Yankees. I don't like to see him retire."

"If I had his body," said about Clemente, "I would keep on playing. Unfortunately, I don't. There's a time for everybody to quit. Mine is here."

*HISTORICAL DETAILS, INCLUDING GAME COMMENTARY AND PLAYER QUOTES, ARE DRAWN FROM THE PITTSBURGH POST-GAZETTE.

INNOCENTLY TO AMUSE THE IMAGINATION IN THIS DREAM OF LIFE IS WISDOM

Mother agreed to transport Victor Bunce and his flashy green stone fountain pen tucked in his pants pocket across town to take weekly writing lessons from Miss Mumms—a blind senior citizen, who had been the Composition teacher at Our Lady of Perpetual Hell Middle School (actually Our Lady of Perpetual Help Middle School) for 50 years.

Victor had heard lots of stories about Miss Mumms—she was a writing teacher after all—the scariest involved documented incidents of her reading some essay that didn't agree with her sensibilities (usually blasphemy) and latching onto the ears of the bad student essayist, "emancipating" the story-stricken soul from the her classroom, transporting him, in tow, down to the Father Paul's Office, presenting the principal the mind-soiled pages, and washing her hands of the dirty-minded rascal.

These tales were passed around the steepled halls of Our Lady and warned that this girl or that boy who found him or herself in similar straights had better not stop short, or else find themselves earless, holding a batch of red-marked pages in front of Jesus with his thorny crown—an imposing picture that adorned most of the wall of the Front Office.

But these tales were from long ago, and Victor just wanted to learn to compose essays like Montaigne or Emerson or Samuel Johnson. He wanted to do more than just noodle around with his fountain pens, making endless circles and testing the inks while trying to think of something meaningful to write—he wanted to compose something that would do the new ideas in his head justice, like G.K. Chesterton. "The other day, a well-known writer, otherwise quite well-informed, said that the Catholic Church is always the enemy of new ideas. It probably did not occur to him that his own remark was not exactly in the nature of a new idea."[1]

The fountain pens—four of them, one made of burl wood, one of flashy green stone with a silver nib, one with a cylinder as grey as the flecks in his cat Pete's eyes, and the last—yellowish stone made to look like petrified wood—sat silently side-by-side in wooden boxes—tucked tight—their sleek rock-hard surfaces illuminating Victor's imagination. What strange sounds the pens might produce if allowed to match the ambient noises inside his head? Noise, like De Quincey, he was intent upon releasing to the world—or at least to the living room. "But my way of writing is rather to think aloud, and follow my own humours, than much to consider who is listening to me; and, if I stop to consider what is proper to be said to this or that person, I shall soon come to doubt whether any part at all is proper."[2]

Victor imagined penning a great essay and then suddenly pulling open the living room windows and reading it aloud to a silent and appreciative audience of friends, who sat cross-legged like supplicants in his front yard. He especially imagined Heidi Hammer sitting there with legs folded underneath, "enamored" by the words he imagined producing. Heidi Hammer, who he loved more than life itself, with short straight-cut bangs that rose up with each purposeful breath, who sat in the front row of composition class and had read more classic essays than he. Once, on the school bus, she called him

Montaigne and then wrote her number on the palm of his hand with a felt marker. Victor hadn't been able to get home before his sweaty palm eradicated the number into smears. Montaigne indeed: "If you press me to say why I loved [her], I can say no more than it was because [she] was [she] and I was I."[3]

Thank goodness for his "prodigious" memory—a word he'd looked up and carefully defined along with the words "emancipated" and "enamored" (he'd especially enjoyed the E's) on poor Father Demetrius' 7th grade vocabulary worksheets—worksheets his seventh-grade classmates despised with an all-out hatred reserved for Liver Day in the Cafeteria. Now he was in eighth grade, and Father Demetrius' and his discourses on William Hazlitt seemed many essays past. "I have some desire to enjoy the present good, and some fondness for the past; but I am not at all given to build castles in the air, nor to look forward with much confidence or hope to the brilliant illusions held out by the future."[4]

Thus, for all the sound reasons herein "enumerated" (another E-word), Victor Bunce (with fountain pen in pocket) asked his mother to take him to Dogtown's Nursing Home—ironically called Serenity—to meet Miss Mumms for composition lessons. Poor Father Demetrius had sermonized, more than twice, that the proper use of irony was the highest form of intelligence—or was that Emerson on satire? "The religion of one age is the literary entertainment of the next."[5] Victor could never disentangle the difference between irony and satire. Besides, he wasn't going to be afraid of some blind old woman, especially when he had so much inside of him waiting to get out as well as the potential "admiration" and eternal love from Heidi Hammer.

Miss Mumms hated the words "nursing home"—positively hated them—but she had decided, along with her younger sister Ruth, that this "assisted living facility" (now those were more appropriate words) was the best thing for them. What did Twain say, "Age is an issue of mind over matter. If you don't mind, it doesn't matter."[6]

After arriving at Serenity, she and Ruth met pretty much everybody right away: a man who called himself The Mayor, who organized Saturday Night Bingo and made straight the cafeteria lines and organized the folks who fumbled picking up sloppy joe's, turkey tetrazzini, baked fish and Jello cake, helping the infirm place each plated item on their trays with admirable aplomb. (Boy was he bossy with a whistle around his neck, "imploring" everyone to eat all of their vegetables, to wipe their mouths and not to forget to recycle their plasticware.); a lady with a chicken-scratch voice who volunteered to read to them from picture books during Friday Happy Hours—in truth the sour wine was better than her sour voice and the baby books she force-fed them; a woman they all called G-ma, who insisted on reciting each day's date instead of the required breakfast prayers; and, poor Father Demetrius, who still thought he was teaching seventh grade English at "Our Lady" and who sat in his tilted-back Broda wheelchair and was continually correcting the grammar on all of The Mayor's signs. "We all boil at different degrees,"[7] Father would say, giving a nod to Emerson.

Serenity—what a joke, but the food was pretty good, and the nurse (Florence "Nightingale" Gundy) and administrative assistant (Marsha Ruth Rulings) were scrappy enough, but one still had to watch them. The two sisters didn't really have much worth stealing, having long ago given almost all of their valuables away, except for Nuna's big bed, heavy as ore that they'd had, through the will of God, moved into Miss Mumms' room.

Collectively, the sisters worried the huge bed wouldn't fit through the doorway but suspected that because of the pretty-penny they were spending to live in Serenity that those in charge weren't in any position to deny them much of anything (including cutting a bigger doorway), and they figured if it took a crane to hall the four-post up and through their window, then so be it.

Although Ruth secretly wished for the chaos, there were more pragmatic ways to get the old bed into the room. And Miss Mumms had so loved to write in bed and then sleep like Virginia Woolf: "We are become part of that unfeeling universe that sleeps when we at our quickest and burns red when we lie asleep."[8] And writing in bed, "never a bad place to write,"[9] scratching in the journals she'd used to compose her days. "A woman must have money and a room of her own to write..."[10]

Still, she and Ruth worried when the workman carried the disassembled pieces of Nuna's fragile wooden bed into her room and whether those clod-footed men would ever be able to put the bed back together again. And ironically, the same day Lady Chicken Scratch read Humpty Dumpty to them.

Of the two sisters, Miss Mumms usually worried the

most, even when Ruth told her all of the worry in the world never amounted to anything. Miss Mumms couldn't help herself. Even after Nuna's old bed was properly put back together, and she told herself to stop worrying she could not will herself to do so. What did the venerable William Hazlitt say? "The art of life is to know how to enjoy a little and to endure very much."[11]

Victor's mother's Taurus found its way around Serenity's circular drive and dropped him off at the front door. He pushed the green button on the outside wall and made his way to the front desk and signed-in.

He had just learned to sign his name in new American cursive and was rather proud of his signature. The lady wearing white and a chartreuse hairnet, nametag Marsha Ruth Rulings, sat behind the "implacable" desk, and watched the corner television with the concentration of a scientist. She never looked up when he appeared in front of her but told Victor to sit in one of the plastic fishbowl lobby window seats adjacent to the front door and wait.

Victor tried to ignore all of the things around him that reeked of "infirmity." Walkers huddled into numbered miniature parking spaces near the front desk awaiting drivers; plastic bags filled with who knew what dangling from metal hooks above the walkers; coffee table books (never opened) "replete" with pictures of rose gardens and historic homes and rooms in the Governor's mansion; two orange neon golf carts, parked in their own spaces outside seemed to be the preferred method of travel. And there were snacks but not the kind of snacks that should be called snacks: apple juice, granola bars, fat-free chips, Gas X tablets, and a bunch of fiber cookies. Where was De Quincey when one needed him? "That those eat now who never ate before."[12]

Unlike many teachers, Miss Mumms never believed in transcendence through her students. She had more modest hopes. She'd oft-quoted Emerson to them, "Let us unlearn our wisdom of the world. Let us lie low in the Lord's power and learn that truth alone makes rich and great."[13]

This new student, for instance, what was his name? Buncie? would undoubtedly let her down, just like all of the others who used to come into class after missing a week, hand her a sick note, and ask her if they'd done anything. Her practiced response, "No, we were waiting for your return before we would dare even open our hymnals."

In truth, Miss Mumms was slightly nervous about teaching Buncie. She hadn't taught in a long time nor written a word since both her eyes had given way six months ago.

It was time to pick up the chalk. To make herself whole again. Where was Hazlitt when one needed him? "We do not see nature with our eyes, but with our understandings and our hearts."[14]

The heart of the matter was that one couldn't get used to just about anything, and some things one didn't want to get used to. Nothing in life seemed to be fair, but unlike Chesterton, and his views on perfectionism, "If a thing is worth doing, it is worth doing badly,"[15] she, a perfectionist, was always prepared to be disappointed.

"Blessed is he who expecteth nothing, for he shall enjoy everything."[16]

Ruth oft-quoted George Santayana with emendations from Churchill and Marx: "Those who cannot remember the past are condemned to repeat it."[17] It was true, as sure as a Hallmark Card. And Miss Mumms hated Hallmark cards. Threw them in the trash before she even opened them, supplying Vonnegut's retort to the Ruth's perineal aphorisms: "Why me? Why you? Why us for that matter? Why anything?"[18] If Ruth repeated that thing about bad things happening to good people one more time, she swore on a stack of Tums, she would never talk to her sister for the rest of the month—which might very well be a lifetime.

She one hundred, Ruth ninety-eight. No matter how one calculates a life—through work, through children, through accomplishments, through successful pupils, through money, through time—none of it was enough. Why hadn't old people produced a handbook for living that said so?

What mattered? Chinese food, having her hair done every week, listening to the BBC World News, The Mayor, who had taken a liking to her and who forgave her when she cut in line, cheated in Bingo, and who even gave her extra candy bars, which she kept stacked on the end of Nuna's bed. Her relationship with The Mayor might well have mattered, but he was only eighty and she was far too mature for that pipe dream.

Victor Bunce sat in that uncomfortable plastic wrap-around seat still and quiet like a church boy for a good long time. The world was sure a funny place and then this: waiting in some circle of hell called Serenity.

Hadn't Dante put some of his teachers in Hell? And were they in Serenity or with the Sodomites? He'd seen Father Demetrius' decline, and then poor Father was whisked away—never to return. Serenity gained? Certainly, lost. Hey, that was a funny one, but nobody seemed to be laughing here, not even Milton. "And may at last my weary age. Find out the peaceful hermitage."[19]

After taking that infernal medicine, her vision had turned blurry and then to half-shadows. She made the grave mistake of not telling anyone—not even Ruth, who admonished her in her dreams. And by the time she had stopped the medicine, her vision was all but gone. "I become a transparent eyeball. I am nothing."[20] And like Emerson, she felt like nothing. Who was an English teacher without eyes? Without being able to see?

Why? Why? Why? Why had she continued taking that damned medicine even long after her vision had turned blurry? Why her, indeed? She knew better than to trust others who couldn't imagine being inside her 100-year-old bones. She understood what it meant to be sixty-five or seventy or ninety-five or even ninety-nine, but no one, especially not the doctors or nurses or pharmacists had any idea what it was like to live a century.

What was it about her need to comply? To "acquiesce"? Everyone thought her difficult, everyone, and when it came to teaching, maybe she had been, but not when it came to listening to others who were paid to care: Doctors. Nurses. Maybe real caring was too much to ask. Too much to hope for.

Ruth assured her that her vision would come back—promised even—and she waited. Turned into a nervous wreck daily as she relived her own mistakes. But blame wasn't a fixer.

Was something seriously wrong with her judgment? Everyone came to her for advice. Yet, why wasn't she good at taking her own? So said Twain, "A man cannot be comfortable without his own approval."[21] Or was it the social contract? "Every man having been born free and master of himself, no one else may under any pretext whatever subject him without his consent."[22] Thank you, Rousseau.

Now, blind, she didn't know what to think about any of it: her vision, about the years spent teaching, about the four-post bed, about Serenity itself—what had Ruth always said plain as day? "God never gives you more than you can handle and never any more than you can stand."

Maybe poor Father Demetrius had a sermon on it somewhere in those sermons written on yellow legal pads now stacked to the ceiling of his room. He said he was going to type them up one day, make a book. Miss Mumms knew he never would in a thousand years if he had them. No, poor Father Demetrius would be forever content re-reading the stack of legal pads filled with his writing, and, in doing so, allow himself to imagine that he had accomplished something. And soon those sermons would be gone, poured into a large trash can.

A lady in sunglasses with a walking stick, whose polished handle was in the shape of a ukulele, suddenly appeared in front of Victor. She waited for him to stand up and held out her frail hand before she spoke. Between the time he stood up and took Miss Mumm's hand, Victor wondered where life would find him in ninety years.

"Come now, young Buncie," Miss Mumms said. "This day is desperately sad, but there is the distinct possibility it will open up to us." As she held his hand, her uke-stick tapped its way toward the Rec. Room; they passed the doors of each resident—most of whom sat in profile and uncertainty in front of flickering television screens. She said, "'To die is not to begin to die, and continue; it is not a state of continuance, but of transientness'[23]—let's thank Thoreau."

All this talk about death. Victor didn't know if he could take it.

In the Rec. Room, Miss Mumms tapped her cane and bade him sit. The organ bench was hard and hurt his bum, and the organ was impossibly old with a wooden finish and as tall as blazes. It looked like it was about to rise up out of the floor and command the situation like a king or a duke that one should bow down to.

He sat silently; his imagination competing with the commanding instruments' magical knobs, switches, keys, petals, and flashing lights. "Buncie, stop playing with the switches—although I know it's tempting, we need to work on your attitude about writing. That's the first thing."

Then Miss Mumms was suddenly sitting on the left side of him. He breathed in the different arthritis rubs Miss Mumms applied daily and felt very small sitting in front of the organ and believed that it might be better if he stood, but it was as if his feet were stuck like pudding to the floor. While sitting beside Miss Mumms, her arm almost touching his—and, oh, that smile of perpetual disappointment—her, just sitting there, waiting for what? For Chesterton? "Around every corner is another gift waiting to surprise us, and it will surprise us if we can achieve control over our natural tendencies to make comparisons, to take things for granted and to feel entitled."[24]

"Let's acquaint ourselves with silence, shall we, Buncie? Too often we try to compose before we listen."

Victor sat there in front of the imposing organ, very much memorizing the two pump pedals covered with red carpet and looked into the large, distorted mirror, which framed the top of the organ. Why hadn't he noticed it before? Victor didn't like the look of himself, as if he had suddenly become old.

"Remember, Samuel Johnson, 'Silence propagates itself, and the longer talk has been suspended, the more difficult it is to find anything to say,'"[25] Miss Mumms continued: "That silence, listen to it, Buncie. Everything that you need to learn about writing is in that silence. Try to listen with your eyes before you feel the words with your fingers—that's the second thing."

And here poor Father Demetrius came—Florence "Nightingale" Gundy pushing his wheelchair and sitting him right next to the organ on Victor's right. Father Demetrius, continually taking off his socks, trying to get up from his chair.

Why had Miss Mumms brought Father here? Victor had heard in some recessed corner that Father

Demetrius had fallen, taken ill, been put in this old folks' home. Poor Father Demetrius—there he was looking at Victor's reflection but not really looking at him—his beard shaved—and when the nurse had presented him, Victor wasn't quite sure who he was looking at, and he'd become very familiar with Father Demetrius, who appeared in his seventh-grade nightmares. There was one particular dream that Victor kept having throughout his seventh-grade school year. Victor could see every speck of Father's classroom in his mind's eye—a very rectangular space, the Websters' perfectly aligned with the edges of the shelves in the back-bottom of the room. In the dream, Victor was certain that Father had placed the reference books there on those lowly shelves to ensure they were nearly impossible to get to out of some strange belief that if the dictionaries were hidden away, they would seem more alluring to kids. Yet, the assignment was due, and Victor couldn't complete it. Father Demetrius didn't understand that kids were not interested in ignoring things that were difficult to get to. And Victor who couldn't remember if Cicero's structure was in five or six parts, and in his dream, Father had turned on him and said, "More is lost by indecision than wrong decision. Indecision is the thief of opportunity. It will steal you blind."[26] Poor Father Demetrious, who was now tilted upward in that hospice wheelchair, his shirt wrapped around his head.

Miss Mumms thought poor Father Demetrius would provide the familiar for Buncie—enlighten him with Hazlitt on language. Father picked up a yellow legal pad from his lap and began: "On the contrary," he said, "there is nothing either musical or natural in the ordinary construction of language. It is a thing altogether arbitrary and conventional."[27] Miss Mumms cocked her eyebrow. "Arbitrary and conventional," he repeated, "Neither in the sounds themselves, which are the voluntary signs of certain ideas, nor in their grammatical arrangements in common speech, is there any principle of natural imitation, or correspondence to the individual ideas, or to the tone of feeling with which they are conveyed to others."[28]

No, poor Father Demetrius would be forever content reading from the stack of legal pads filled with his writing, and, in doing so, allow himself to imagine that he had accomplished something. And his reciting Hazlitt was gone like the Cheetos he put out for Bingo. He might as well eat the bag. "The jerks, the breaks, the inequalities, and harshness of prose are fatal to the flow of poetical imagination, as a jolting road or stumbling horse disturbs the reverie of an absent man."[29] Father became agitated and took off his socks and tried again to get out of his chair. Poor Father Demetrius was nothing else if not persistent, and Miss Mumms was afraid that finally he would make it to his feet and topple to the floor. What was this implacable need to constantly fill the silence with one's own breath?

So, there they all sat looking into the mirror at each other. But Miss Mumms couldn't see herself and poor Father Demetris lay tilted back in his Broda chair, the drip bag above his head, its plastic coiling into his arm. And what were those great essays and what made a great essayist? Hazlitt, Twain, Emerson, Johnson,

Chesterton? That's what Father Demetrius used to ask them while they sat fidgeting in his class. What would he say? "They were marking the signposts—visiting islands—finding the connective tissue—interstices—joints in between." Father took pleasure in striking through incorrect vocabulary words and held his own pen just so—who taught them that letters needed to appear to be the same height. "So says Hazlitt, 'But poetry makes these odds all even. It is the music of the language answering to the music of the mind, untying as it were the 'secret soul of harmony.'"[30] Poor Father Demetrius, poor Miss Mumms, who cautioned that all the style in the world didn't mean much if one didn't have anything to say. To paraphrase Twain, who wrote: "Anybody can have ideas—the difficulty is to express them without squandering a quire of paper on an idea that ought to be reduced to one glittering paragraph."[31] And this not having anything important to say was what Victor feared most—all of the handwriting exercises in the world meant little if this—what was presented in front of him was what it all came to—how it all ended up.

As if on cue, Victor produced the green fountain pen from his pocket and held it up high. He looked to the mirror as his fountain penned hand descended upon the keys. A single note on the organ bounced off the empty Rec. Room furniture.

And Miss Mumms began: "We forget ourselves and our destinies in health, and the chief use of temporary sickness is to remind us of these concerns."[32] And Ralph Waldo Emerson with his beaky nose, penetrating eyes and school master's collar appeared beside her in the mirror.

Father Demetrius answered, "We are fonder of visiting our friends in health than in sickness. We judge less favorably of their characters when any misfortune happens to them; and a lucky hit, either in business or reputation, improves even their personal appearance in our eyes."[33] And the young-looking William Hazlitt, his neck wrapped in a protruding collar, as if right out of seventh grade, appeared beside Father Demetrius in the mirror.

"The mere pursuit of health always leads to something unhealthy. Physical nature must not be made the direct object of obedience; it must be enjoyed not worshipped,"[34] said Miss Mumms, who conjured G.K. Chesterton, who in middle age with those glasses, mustache and tie appeared in the mirror with a wry smile on his face.

And like a tennis match, Father Demetrius volleyed back, "Health is so necessary to all the duties, as well as pleasure of life, that the crime of squandering is equal to folly."[35] Wigged, white-haired, imposing Samuel Johnson, with a perpetual scowl filled the mirror.

Finally, Miss Mumms put the game away with Twain, "The only way to keep your health is to heade what you don't want, drink what you don't like and do what you'd druther not."[36] In a white suit, Mark Twain appeared in the mirror smiling.

And, for a moment, there was a perfect tableau. A picture framed from long ago. The past and the present along with each other. And Florence Nightingale Grundy, who had been standing in the background during these exchanges, fumbled in her pocket and extricated a camera with a flash. "Smile," she said and the flashbulb hit the mirror in a blast of white blinding light.

And, afterwards, in the mirror were only the three of them.

"Whenever I want to be done with an essay, Buncie. Whenever I want it to be over—that's exactly the time when I need to go back in. That's when it's not done at all. Don't you see? That's when it's not done at all. Remember the poet Yeats, Buncie: 'Only that which does not teach, which does not cry out, which does not persuade, which does not condescend, which does not explain is irresistible."[37]

And Victor presented his flashy green stone fountain pen with the silver nib to Miss Mumms at the end of this, his first composition lesson.

A PEBBLE AT DAWN

What most disturbed Ben Sykes about his present situation was how it had crept up on him: Ben had lost his home, his wife, and he had thrown away his job. He wasn't able to say which one thing brought him to this—the world was certainly a more complex and complicated place than placing blame on one thing. If it wasn't for his ex-mother-in-law, Mrs. Edna Ferbish, allowing Ben to stay with her, well.

Edna had always liked Ben. She doted on him far more than Jonelle, her daughter, whom Edna fought with like a cat. "Two women cannot co-exist in the same house," Edna had told him. "Beware, Ben. This is an incontrovertible truth."

Soon after Ben began living with Edna, he noticed her hatred of traditional holidays. On Christmas, for instance, there was no tree, no stockings, no lights, no bread pudding, no fruit cake, no mistletoe—instead, they ordered Wok & Roll: bourbon chicken, fried rice, and cold sesame noodles. The New Year went unacknowledged, too; there was no sparkling wine, no popping of corks, no throw-away plastic cups, no pointy hats, no air horns, no streamers—there was no pork and sauerkraut, either. Instead, Edna made corn dogs on a stick and poured Ben a Coke.

Similarly, there were no Easter eggs, no baskets, no fake grass, no bonnets, no Easter dresses, no Cadbury Eggs; there were never birthday cakes, and forget about candles.

Edna did, however, acknowledge Memorial Day, D-Day, Armistice Day, and the day the Gulf of Tonkin Resolution was signed. She wore an armband to celebrate V-J Day; however, she busily crossed her arms, begrudging the date of the Cuban Missile Crisis, saying it wasn't a real holiday. From a distance, perhaps, only acknowledging war holidays was something that Ben hoped to be able to laugh at later. But Thanksgiving dinner was still spaghetti at the Gab & Eat, and the year passed without a single resolution.

Ben tried to celebrate in little ways: he bought a good, processed turkey, but Edna fed it to the birds; he brought a poinsettia, but Edna set it ablaze and left it burning on the porch; he dragged into the house a little Christmas tree, but Edna sawed in two with a Shun knife.

"I took a test at the Senior Center on the Interweb, and I've learned I'm in the 3rd circle of Hell," Edna announced one day in May. Then she followed up and said, "Can a woman rightly be called a dick? That's what Karen Knoll called me while there."

Ben Sykes spent a great deal of time trying to figure out what was wrong with his ex-mother-in-law but soon began to realize, all things being equal, the simplest answer was most likely: she was crazy as a cartoon. He made an appointment with Dr. Mitchell.

"Complicity and duplicity," Edna said over-and-over after Ben Sykes had managed to coerce her out of the house, "D-Day is on the way, Ben, and I have to attend to setting up the tubs for the boats and soldiers."

The television remained eternally on and very loud. As a joke, Ben bought a pointy foil hat for the anniversary of the Nuclear Test Ban Treaty, but Edna said, "Live free or die," and tossed the hat into the fireplace and poured on the creosote.

In late August when they pulled up in front of a rather nondescript building, Edna refused to get out of the car—wouldn't unbuckle her seat belt. "Don't imagine that I don't know exactly how this looks, but I don't quite see how even my own ex-son-in-law can make me go in there. It's not like I've violated parole." Edna sat in the car for about fifteen minutes, staring ahead and not acknowledging him. Then, she opened the car window and yelled at the building, "This used to be in the same spot where they made Talk-of-the-Town Bread. Sometimes the loaves arrived at the store so fresh that the bread was still warm within the plastic wrapper." With that, Edna closed the window and said, "Let's reschedule this shrink-wrapped visit, Ben. I'll promise you I'll go in next time if we can drive away to the Gab & Eat. I have a hankering for butter squash soup and rare roast beef on multi-grained bread."

On the second visit, Edna said she was too embarrassed to eat the brown bag lunch Ben had packed: a grilled cheese sandwich, an orange and hard-boiled egg with a small packet of salt. Edna remained in the car and said, "Doctor Bedbug will think I'm an immigrant eating congealed American cheese on toast that tastes just like flesh!"

"On the third trip, Ben stood under a large emblematic umbrella out in the rain while Edna spit out the side window of the car and recounted how she always pickled relish as a sandwich spread on Memorial Day. Then, she mused aloud that her pickled sandwich spread had clogged a lot of hearts.

On the fourth visit, Edna talked about how in the eighth grade, she had developed a taste for eating crayons, as many as twenty in one sitting. "I still sometimes go to the Dollar Store and drool," she said, "and sometimes I still can't resist chewing on colored paper."

One day in early October after a particularly violent storm, Ben Sykes returned home to find their outdoor garage had blown down. Edna stood at the screened door and said, "Thank God for large and small miracles —for crayons and waxed paper and clichés, and Ben watch out for that sinkhole the rain seems to have uncovered."

Ben tried to fill in the large and scary sinkhole, but the dirt he pitched in was immediately swallowed up with no end in sight. "Did you use calcified dirt or gravel?" Edna said when Ben, dirty and disheveled, found his way to the table for dinner: "Gravel is in the garage; I should have told you before."

As the days passed, Edna seemed to remember more about the past and observe less of the present. She couldn't remember her pill schedule but could remember recipes of long-lost pies and breads and miscellaneous facts about her family history. "One signed the Declaration of Independence, and the other didn't see fit to allow black and white children in the same schools. I'm here to tell you, Ben. I'm proud and not proud of it all." No detail escaped her: an errant thread on Ben's shirt was snapped off like a spider web, a button about to lose itself was plucked off his coat like a wandering eye, and in-seams were redoubled before they tore free. Ben found Edna's triumphs of attention to the future's little disasters all rather disturbing. And he was embarrassed the fifth time he had to cancel on Dr. Bedbug. The receptionist, who had been rather kind and understanding of the four previous cancellations, said, "You know, Mr. Sykes, each cancellation on Dr. Mitchell comes with a charge, and up until this time, I was able to wave the fee, but I'm just not going to be able to do that anymore. We have the right to refuse service!"

Ben Sykes knew Edna would eternally refuse to get out of the car, but he continued to drive her out to the nondescript building. Predictably, his ex-mother-in-law would make up some excuse, refuse to take off her seat belt, and, then, after about fifteen minutes and another story about bread, together they would go to the Gab & Eat.

Ben actually worried that one day Edna might run out of stories about pies (Rhubarb, Custard, Snowball) and bread (Pineapple, Ginger and something she called

Aloft) and forget why she came and suddenly get out of the car. And in this worry, Ben Sykes began to realize that he had not-so-suddenly become a middle-aged man, who lived with his ex-mother–in-law. He was afraid this fact would overshadow all that he might well in the future accomplish.

"I've lived in this house for going on sixty years and have decided that I will die here," Edna said while she stood in the small hallway during an undecorated Halloween. No candy, no rubber bats, no plastic pumpkins filled to the brim with fun-size candy—"Nothing fun about 'em," Edna said after ignoring another knock at the door. "I just wanted you to know about the dying part, Ben because I don't think that I have said that before."

Ben had an ornery streak when it came to the Kingdom of Death, yet he tried to curb this instinct and said, "Just smile and keep quiet, Mom. The trick-or-treaters you're ignoring will know we're in here and toilet paper and egg the house." Through the symbolic gesture of his empty hands, Ben tried to prove that he, unlike the hooligans waiting with open maws for fun-size bars, meant no harm.

"You have a mean streak, Ben," was all that Edna said.

One evening to celebrate Liberation Day, they went to a fancy Italian Restaurant two towns away. Edna complained about the uncomfortable plastic wicker chairs and refused to eat her Bolognese when she overheard a thin man who stood at the front door say that his wife was presently in the emergency room having her stomach pumped after having had a reaction to the sauce. Edna's dinner sat there congealing while Ben ate the salad, his pasta, two orders of bread, and gelato.

Edna watched him eat and said, "I don't want to make a scene, Ben." Then she had the nice waiter wrap up her dinner and promptly she disposed of it, dropping it into the first receptacle she could find on the street.

Notes from Tennis Camp

monday:

I like bugs. I hate my dad's clothes 'cause he always wears brown. I like the tennis coach 'cause he's blond, wears a color that's not brown, and has a nice voice, soft, that tells funny stories. I like the tennis balls 'cause they're yellow, and when I hold two of them up to my eyes and yell, "I'm a bug!" everybody at tennis camp laughs. I like the tennis courts 'cause they're green, red, and white, but the truth is—I hate tennis. I'd rather sit under the big tree outside the pretty courts and watch the bugs take flying lessons from their Ma's and Pa's. I don't even think I should be playing tennis 'cause I got a hole in my heart.

The doctor said I could never play three sports: football, motorcycles, and skiing. I wish the doctor would have said no tennis, but he didn't, and here I am.

Ace V. Love, the tennis coach, starts camp by making us call out numbers real loud. I'm a number one. Shannon Carriage, my next-door neighbor, is a number two. Shannon tells Ace she doesn't want to be number two. So, we switch.

Ace always hits the ball before I'm ready. "Pal," he says, "you got to turn your body this way." "Pal," he shouts, "you got to turn your body that way." "Pal," he yells, "pay attention and move those feet."

"Alan Meeks," he says, "you run slower than water uphill."

Ace V. Love only calls me by my full name when he's disappointed in me. The rest of the time, he calls me Meeks.

"Meeks," he says, "I hope you're ready. Here comes the smoker, the whizzer, the demon speedball." Then, Ace hits the ball before I'm ready. "Swing, Meeks!" he shouts. "And a miss! Strike one! That's okay, you have two more chances. Ready position? Here comes the supersonic-underhanded sinker. Are you ready? Swing, Meeks!" he yells. "Striiiiike two! You can do this, Alan. I want you to concentrate. Ready position? Okay, here comes the skinny-fat ball guaranteed to make mountains outta' mole hills and boys into men. Swing!" I close my eyes and hit the ball hard. My hand goes wobbly. "And you can kiss it goodbye!" Ace yells into the handle of his racket. "The crowd goes wild," Ace makes all these hissing sounds and claps the strings of his racket against his hand. "A grand slam for Alan 'The Squeak' Meeks. Now, Meeks, you know what this powerful display of brute force means?"

"What?" I say.

"It's time for you to tie your laces and run the paces around the bases."

I drop my racket and run after the ball. I can't find it right away. Bugs in the tall weeds are much more interesting. "Where is it, Pal?" Ace asks when I come back to the fence.

"What?"

"The ball, Meeks. Put away your butterflies and welcome to tennis camp!"

tuesday:

Today, I tried to capture a dead dragonfly that had fallen into the sewer grate outside the tennis courts. Dragonflies are long ants with see-thru wings like miracle windows. As soon as I saw the dragonfly, I knew I had to have it for my collection.

My fingers got stuck in the grate. I didn't want to tell anyone, especially Ace. Everyone on the courts stopped playing when I yelled, and then there was a long nothing when Ace tried to pull my fingers out of the grate, but they just wouldn't budge. "This is worse than wearing a wedding ring, huh, Meeks?" Ace said.

Ace had to call to the two big construction workers who stood tall on the buildings across the street and wear ugly-yellow to pick up the grate with my fingers still holding the dragonfly.

They carried me away to the Y.M.C.A. building on the hill. Ace held me in his arms while the two men held the grate in their hands. They sat me down on a long blue couch. One of the men held the grate while the other sat beside me. They said things like, "I can't hear myself think!" and "Could you yell any louder?"

Finally, Ace stopped talking into the phone, put money into a big glass machine, and bought me a Mr. Good candy bar. "Know why they call it Mr. Good, Meeks?"

"It's good!"

"It won't be long now," Ace said when the Janitor came with the saw.

The saw made gritty sounds against the grate. I kept thinking the saw was going to cut through the grate and my fingers and then through the dragonfly. The yellow-men told me if I didn't stop yelling, they were going to pull out my tongue and wrap it around my head.

The dragonfly's wide see-thru wings fell onto the floor and turned to dust. The Janitor holding the coping saw stepped on them with his tired work boots when he left. So did the yellow-men who each held half a grate. I almost cried out but didn't want the yellow-men to start yelling again. I just put another piece of Mr. Good in my mouth, and I held onto the long body of the dragonfly while Heather, the YMCA assistant, told me she was calling home to tell my parents that I needed to get a tetanus shot.

wednesday:

I think my dad hates the tennis coach. I know it's my fault he hates him. When he got home from work last night, I lied about my fingers and how they got hurt. I told Dad I fell on the top of a tennis can lid that was metal and rusty and lying on the tennis courts. On our way to the hospital to get a tetanus shot, Dad asked how old Ace V. Love was and if he paid attention to us.

Today, Ace was late to Tennis Camp. He told us he got a flat tire before practice. He said he accidentally hit the curb outside the Y.M.C.A. building 'cause he was watching Heather Lockjaw walk and not what he was doing. "But it was worth it, Pal!" he said and hit a tennis ball at me before I was ready, and I swung too hard and hit it over the fence again.

When I ran outside after it, I noticed a big board over

the grate. Ace told me not to go near it. He said he didn't want me falling into the sewer. "Raccoons live down there," he said, and if I didn't like tetanus shots, I would hate rabies shots 'cause the needles are as long as his arm.

At lunch, while we all sat under the big tree, I shook up my tennis ball container filled with grape Kool-Aid mixed with one tablespoon of sugar and pool water.

"Yum! It tastes just like soda pop."

Ace said it's not safe to drink pool water, no matter how good it tastes. He said it could make me puke. He said if I fell down and foamed at the mouth, he would have to take me to the hospital to get my stomach pumped. "Have you ever had your stomach pumped, Meeks?"

"No!" I said, "but I swallowed a yellow jacket once."

"Then your stomach must have a pretty good lining."

He's not very smart, the tennis coach. Then, he told us that we should always be sure to watch where we are going and never-ever to drive under the influence of pool water. "Oooops," he said, "I shouldn't have told you that. Now, you're all going to go home and drive your tricycles under the influence of pool water, and you're only eight years old. I feel miserable."

Shannon said, "We don't ride tricycles anymore, Ace."

"I still feel miserable," he said and pointed to his car. "That tire is going to cost me big bucks."

thursday:

Today, I decided to like Shannon Carriage. She's a girl, but I decided to like her anyway. I chased her around the red areas of the tennis courts and threw pollen at her. She screamed, "Jerk!" and hit me in the face with the ball.

Because it was hot, Ace let us play Water Tennis. We were supposed to yell, "You're the ball," and squirt water from our water-sippers at each other. I tried to squirt Shannon, but I missed every time. Then, for fun, I stuck the plastic straw from my water-sipper into my heart-scar and yelled, "I've been strawed through the heart." Everyone at tennis camp laughed, except for Ace. He just took my water sipper away.

At lunch, I gave Ace half of my Fluffer-Nutter-peanut butter and banana sandwich. Ace just stared at it and then opened it up to see what was inside. I sat down next to him under the big tree and told him that the female bug is the one who bites, and the male bug is the one who stays at home to protect the eggs.

"Male bugs have it good. Don't ya' think, Meeks?" he whispered and took a bite of his Fluffer-Nutter.

I told him that after the female bug bites you, she carries your skin home to feed her babies. He asked me if I still liked Shannon after what I just said about female bugs. "Yep," I said, "Women are pretty aggressive."

"Yep," he said, "Women can be pretty complex."

"And I've discovered they don't like water."

friday:

This is the last day of tennis camp. Ace says we will have a pizza party after the tournament. Yum. I like pizza.

In the morning, Dad comes down to the tennis courts in his brown suit to watch me play in the first round. Dad stands tall with his fingers in the fence while Shannon serves the ball over and over again and again. "40 Love," Shannon yells real loud and hits the ball extra hard.

"Out," Dad yells.

"It's your call, Pal," Ace says real nice to me.

"It was in. Good game, Shannon," I say, lock eyes with Dad, and hit one final ball over the fence on purpose and into the weeds.

Dad turns his back and watches the ball fly high over his head. I think he's going to run after it so we can find bugs together in the tall weeds, but he just waves goodbye and slowly walks away to his car. At the net, I shake hands with Shannon, who says, "Good game, Meeks. Too bad your dad didn't stay for Pizza," and rubs her fists into her eyes and yells, "I'm a ladybug."

Right before lunch, Ace picks me up on his back. I hang around his neck. "We are on a jungle safari, Meeks," he says. "Get the big nets ready for the Zebra swallowtail."

"Look," I say, "it's a rare and tasty Pizza Mantis!"

The pizza delivery man doesn't even smile, he just stands in front of Ace holding the boxes.

Today, lunch is the best ever. Ace sits under the big tree outside the tennis courts with me while the others play in the tournament. We count the bugs in the sky. I call them out by name real fast: "Black-winged damselfly, two-striped grasshopper, June bug, and buffalo treehopper."

Ace says, "Flying bug number 1, jumping bug number 2, squatting bug number 3, big ugly bug number 4."

Ace points to the big scar on my chest where they tried to fix the hole in my heart and asks me if it hurts.

"It did, but it doesn't," I say.

"Mine too, Meeks." He stares at his car, and I stare at the board over the sewer grate.

I don't think I will ever forget tennis camp. I tell Ace that I love him like a bug and put the tennis balls up to my eyes for the last time.

"Finish your pizza, Meeks," he says and hands me a Mr. Good out of his big bag.

SCREECH AND THE DARK-SHIRTED STREETS

Phase 1

Screech and his best friend Sammer were alone on the dark-shirted streets of the Southside of Pittsburgh. Their fathers had warned them many times not to fool around on these streets because they were very dangerous and told them never to wear black T's in this dark because something terrible might happen.

Tonight was the 4th of July—a full year after Screech's father had passed—and the hullabaloo of Pittsburgh's annual fireworks display was in session.

River barges sent skyward a monumental display, but tonight, of all summer nights, there was a low cloud ceiling. The smoke lay heavy like a solid in the sky and forced the asthmatic Sammer to catch his breath and try to hold onto it, but the air kept seeping through his fingers.

Sammer had what Screech called "convenient asthma." Tonight, though, the smoke found its way into both of their lungs, and this was a smoke that didn't let go, a smoke that you never really got used to—not even when immersed in it.

With the current July 4th traffic buzzing and bolting and swearing and swerving all around them, Screech, purposely clad in a dark T, as near as Sammer could tell in the dark, pulled Rusted Red with THE BIG SUCKER trailing toward the doorless doorway of the 333 Bar & Grill.

Screech's father had warned them many times in "NO UNCERTAIN TERMS" to stay out of the 333 Bar & Grill because of the men with skull finger rings and women with stick knives, both, who sidled belly-up to the 100-year-old oak slab bar that Sammer's daddy and Screech's father had carved their initials in during long-ago-drunken-friendship days.

As Screech stood mute, holding the handle of Rusted Red in front of the open 333 doorway, he glimpsed big neighborhood meanies' fat bums that spilled over the red stools and women's faded lips that tasted the best pickled eggs in the city.

TOMMY 25 and his father Straight 50 kept the pickled eggs in a big jar, filled to the brim with suspicious red liquid. The 333's interior stretched back into unknown shadows, doubling and tripling up on themselves like in a barbershop mirror. Screech heard there was a whole upstairs to the 333 Bar & Grill, where 'dirty things' happened between mens and womens.

Damning the lonely river barges that hummed across the river behind them, Screech left Sammer outside with

Rusted Red and slipped inside the doorless doorway; skittered across the floor like a cockroach; skirted past the fatty bum cracks and yapping lipsticklesslips; slinked into a corner and waitedwaitedwaited.

TOMMY 25 was busy banging on the side of the television; Straight 50, TOMMY 25's father, was monumentally adjusting the rabbit ears and having a time of it, too; quietquietquiet, then Screech manhandled the doorknob that was supposed to lead upstairs to the secret brothel rooms with fabled adornments: silk stocking curtains, red bulbs, strobe lights and lava lamps.

TOMMY 25 yelled, "Git the fuck away from that door, Screech, or I'll give you something to moan about!" Screech was forced to skedaddle, but knew if Straight 50 was in good spirits, the old codger would chuck a pickled egg at his pie-hole as he ran back toward the doorless doorway.

Purple eggs sometimes found the floor—which was horror-gross, but 333 pickled eggs were worth eating at almost any cost. Legend had it Straight 50 used to pitch professionally and had learned his craft from Elroy Face. Yep, Straight 50 could put sidespin on a pickled egg so it curved in the air and wedged right between yer teeth.

"Belly on up to the bar," Straight 50 said while Screech was picking up the last bit of purple egg from the floor and licking his phalanges. "Never be afraid, young man, to name yer' poison," Straight 50 said. "Your father liked A-Drop-of-the-Irish, every now and again."

"And not only after work," TOMMY 25 yelled into the jumping verticals while still banging and adjusting. "Sometimes anytime is all the time for a Tootsie."

Straight 50 reached into the forever-deep glass beside the pickled eggs and plunked down a few of the softest Tootsie Rolls in the city on the hardwood.

"Get on in here, Sammer 'fore the Liquor Control Board shuts us down," TOMMY 25 yelled toward the doorless doorway.

Sammer hesitated. "Are you shittin' me?" TOMMY 25 laughed. "Are you gonna join us like a right-and-regular gentleman or just stand out there holding your handle?"

"Screech and me and Rusted Red are on a very important adventure," Sammer said.

"Well, bring 'er the hell inside," TOMMIE 25 said.

"The 333 is filled with adventures of all kinds," Kind Annie laughed. Kind Annie laughed most of the time TOMMIE 25 did anything, including parting his hair.

Sammer rolled Rusted Red in over knotted floorboards so grey it was hard to imagine there was wood under the dirt.

"The BIG SUCKER HAS ARRIVED," Ben Birthright said.

"Jesus H. Christ, Sammer. Is that a rocket or a bomb?" Kind Annie's eyes got real big.

"It's a fuckin' prop," Ben Birthright said.

"So, you boys intend on lightin' that firecracker or yenz just wheelin' it around to make up for what you ain't got in your pants?" TOMMY 25 gave the television another good crack.

Sammer left Big Red just inside and sidled up to the bar next to Kind Annie, who only wore velour dresses and had three teeth. "Hey, Sammer," Kind Annie said, "How's it doin?"

"Sammer, ya jag-off, you didn't shut the door. Yenz going to let out all the air-conditioning or what?" TOMMY 25 smiled at Screech, implicating him, too.

"A Pepper," Screech said forcefully, tracing the curve of the wooden bar. "Ah, 50, go on and slip something in there for the kid," Ben Birthright said. Birthright had a bullethead and used to work coating steel ovens. He had no eyebrows.

"Screech's father liked an Imp and Iron with a shot of Georgia Moon fer an appetizer," Kind Annie said.

"Your Pop, he was, a bullet without a pistol," Birthright said and ran his fingers through his short hair.

"Come over here, both yenz, Straight said for the thousandth time. Trace your fingers in the grooves of the bar here. Yer' Pop, Screech, and that en's carved their names right here in this slab. Don't think it was on the 4th of July, though."

Straight 50 poured out small sips of Iron into the Pepper he kept behind the bar for just such occasions. "Sip 'er fast Sammer. You both got an adventure to get going."

"HOLYMOTHERFUGGINWATERBLESSMEFATHER-FORIHAVESINNED," Screech crossed himself and threw back the Pepper.

Straight 50 put a Dr. Pepper on the bar for Sammer. He pulled the tab with expertise.

"THISLIFETHATAIN'TWORTHLIVINGWITHOUT-THEHAIROFGODBEFOREHEBIT," Sammer crossed and downed the shot.

"With the best of 'em and then some!" Kind Annie pointed to Ben Birthright.

"Now Screech, listen to me. Straight 50 said. Let me tell you a story 'bout yer Pop. One you need to hear. Sammer leave THE BIG FUCKER alone; ain't nobody in here going to steal it."

"The BIG SUCKER," Ben Birthright corrected.

Sammer swiveled back around and shifted his stare to Screech and beside Ben Birthright's eyebrowless eyes.

"Don't stare, kid. It makes me real uncomfortable."

"Now, Screech, here's the straight-up bartender's guide to wisdom and alcohol. So, listen close. The 333's been around 50 years, and this bar slab's been here a lot longer."

"Start 'er off, 50," Kind Annie coaxed.

"Long time ago, the population on the Northside of Pittsburgh was as thick as the smoke on the 4th of July. It was its own city. Trolley cars allowed passengers to hop off, and they'd come in here for lunchtime meals and a beverage; after work, these streets were filled with steel-toed boots and helmets hanging like decapitated yellow Jed's on that wall. The smoke crept up on you like dirty flood water marking each building with a stain.

"Downtawn there were three department stores, three rivers and three professional teams. As a joke, I called this the 333.

"Top of the Gulf building foretold the weather—its orange tiers indicating rain—a blue pyramid suggested uninterrupted grey skies. This city pretends it's a land-locked disaster, but at least we're not Cleveland."

"Hell No!" Ben Birthright chimed in.

"I suppose them three rivers just made us feel sorry for

ourselves for staying behind; who would think of leavin' anyways; we have houses built into these impossible hills; and, we've had great hulks of steel success—each and every mill—even the stainless shops—smoked and carried on in a 'do-it-alone' attitude of a tough town."

"Tell er' right, 50," Kind Annie said.

"Amen," Ben Birthright said.

Sammer squirmed in his seat and looked toward the doorless door. I told ya Sammer to pay attention like your life depended on it and it just well might.

"Screech, we called yer Pop, Feets," Straight 50 said, 'cause he was always on the move in search of big-time adventures. "Used to say 'Feets got feet 'cause he was always runnin.' Called this one's daddy 'Hands' cause he could about make anything, and steam fitted with the best of them. Both would come in here crazy with dirty black mill circles under their eyes. Yep, Feets and Hands every Friday evening one or another holding a bouquet of wild roses. Picked 'em sparingly. Gave the red ones to Kind Annie."

"That's right," Kind Annie smiled.

"Gave the yellow ones to Birthright,"

"Jag-off!" Ben Birthright chuckled.

"We'd put 'em in with the pickled eggs to keep 'em from liltin'."

"Them hairy seeds that got inside tasted bad," Kind Annie said.

"Roses where that jar's sittin', and by the end of the night the rose petals smelled sweet and delicious.

"Feets was always said he 'come in here to find

darkest part 'cause he knew the darkest part was the best," Ben Birthright said.

"Hands was like you Sammer and never said much. Sometimes I think I catch sight of him sittin' in that corner," 50 pointed toward the corner near Rusted Red.

"Keep yer eyes up front here. No use lookin' around for him. He's still here. Take a deepdown-breath." Straight 50 leaned in close to Screech and showed only the whites of his eyes, "'*Spare the rose!—it lives—it lives, / It feels the noon-tide sun, and drinks refresh'd / The dews of night; let not thy gentle hand / Tear sunder...and destroy / The sense of being!—why that infidel smile?*'"[1]

Screech looked quizzically at Sammer.

"We got a big commemorative big-time adventure to get to, Sir."

"This is Phase One. We've planned ahead."

Straight 50 yelled from behind Sammer and his words almost pushed them both out into the dark-shirted streets, "'*And lo! the torch! hold hold your erring hands! / Yet quench the rising flames! —they rise! they spread! / They reach the suffering Maid! oh God protect / The innocent one!*'"[2]

Phase 2

Silent and quick, Screech and Sammer moved through the doorless door and out into the great big wide and wonderful here and now, out beyond the 333 Bar & Grill and found their way across the yellow bridge and into the middle of their big adventure.

Fireworks were illegal in Pennsylvania, but the Pittsburgh cops thought it patriotic on the 4th to look the other way. For Phase Two, Screech and Sammer built this super-crater rocket hat was going to be so fucking loud it had legs. Its fuse was so superscary, you'd have to sit down and strap your shaking legs to a table—to light it.

Together, Screech and Sammer printed THE BIG SUCKER on it in HUGEBIGASSLETTERS.

Deepdeepdeep down in the dark-shirted streets smoke thick in their throats, Screech and Sammer pulled RUSTED RED along with THE BIG SUCKER.

"Let's outsmart 'em all and keep THE BIG SUCKER out in the open. People don't ever pay attention to what's in plain sight," Sammer said.

"Lying doesn't matter much when you never tell the truth in the first place"—at least that's how Screech came to think about it.

Logically, Sammer knew if he was a betting man, he had something to lose if Paradise really did exist, and that the actual and complete end might be today—if they were lucky.

The dark-shirted streets were beginning to find silence, except for their loud-voiced thoughts—the seriousness of their mission, the real chance to blow back the town's eyebrows.

"What's yer favorite dinosaur?" Screech called out as a camel car found its way through the eye of the needle —Sammer's pupil. "Mine's T-Fuckin' Rex."

"Brontosaurus," Sammer said.

"Are you shittin me?"

"They're colossal big."

"They take big dumps, you mean."

Together, Screech and Sammer and RUSTED RED and THE BIG SUCKER crossed busyboulevard and began their upwardclimb under the Mono-Bridge. This was the scary part—only pussies were afraid of the dark.

RUSTED didn't pull well over the gravel and cobblestone unevenness. THE BIG SUCKER threatened to tumble to earth.

"HOLD 'ER STEADY, SAMMER WHILE I NEGOTIATE THE STUBBLE," Screech said in a workmanlike voice.

The cloud covering was so low that they were fully immersed in it as they climbed the Mono-Bridge path toward its apex— Arbuckle Hill—where Screech's father was buried against his will. Mom thought he'd like the constant view, but Screech knew different from the longtalk walks they'd taken together around the world in seventy-five minutes.

The Boulevard itself was still way up above them— its curving lanes flowing like another river, taking all those with it who wanted to exit the city. Cars rumbled, shaking the Mono-Bridge to its stanchions, and for sure the drivers counted the tombstones and concrete crosses, which pointed heavenward but were held down to earth by their weight.

One summer, the Pittsburgh City Council tried to show movies against big solid white sheets they affixed to the stanchions of the Mon-bridge, but the practice was discontinued 'cause religiousitytypes thought showing movies in a cemetery sacrilegious. On Halloween, the kids performed the deathplays. Folks still came out to Arbuckle Hill to watch famous death scenes: Julius Caesar, Romeo and Juliet, MacBeth. Although the Catholic's forever balked, they knew they had used up all their good will when they took shears to the movie screen sheets.

Once Screech tossed condoms filled with Heinz Ketchup off the top of the Mono-bridge just to watch 'em splat. One condom refused to break and rolled along the highway. The little wide-eyed girlies in the cars covered their mouths and pointed from the windows and yelled, "Red cushions rolling dawn the road! Red cushions going to explode."

"I construe myself a cowardly act!" Screech yelled frenetically.

And you can screw THAT Sammer replied without missing a beat.

Certainly, each statement and every word mattered more now with only two hours—or at most three—left in the whole world.

The pavement was uneven near the tip-top of Mono-bridge and these concrete trails had been used by the Irish Steel workers who wound their way down the Mono-hill to the MON mill and later sauntered over to the 333 for spirits.

The MON mill still lay strewn at the bottom of the Mono-hill like an abandoned ship, docked yet disinte-grating. The workers were long gone, but they left arti-facts behind—bottle caps, buttons, clips, steel pennies. Screech and Sammer often brought buckets and brushes to excavate what Screech called in a sullied voice "THE DIG SITE!"

Last time they'd been to visit MON mill, they had unearthed a bottle of Irish Whisky.

The liquid in the bottle was about gone and had congealed into a brown syrup—the bottle must have been 40 years old.

"Wish'en I had a pickled egg to wash down," Screech had said.

"SHIT-Face, it still has a label on it."

And what a pretty bottle it had been—kind of like a flask blown into a swan's neck where you held the sipper.

They flipped the Roberto Clemente card Sammer kept in his pocket for such decision-situations.

As usual, Sammer lost, and yet he kind of won because after Screech sucked on the bottle, he yelled in a manner in which his name had become accustomed, "HOLY GODLESS MOTHER WATER—TASTES-LIKEDIRTANDTURPENTINEANDPUREGOODNESS!"

RUSTED RED moved more slowly than one thought it could.

"Pull the damned thing, Sammer!

My Cathy Helper's starting to blister."

The handle of RUSTED RED felt right in Sammer's hand, like he was hauling something of grave impor-tance. THE BIG SUCKER teetered to its hull.

Screech did not seem overly worried THE BIG SUCKER would topple over.

"You do pull that like you're masturbating," Screech said and lapped at his hand hairs like a cat.

"Speak for yourself, old man."

Clouds were coming in like fog, and the air was heavy with smoke and humidity.

Sammer and Rusted-Red ascended the path, but its flagging wheels felt fixed, anchored to the ground by THE BIG SUCKER.

"I can't see a fuggin' thing, Sammer. How much further ya think?"

Sammer thought about ghosts. Who wouldn't have? He would neverever tell Screech how much he believed in them, nor how much he believed the dead attempted to inform present decisions. Still, Sammer knew to listen to the ghosts when they spoke through neck prickles and with certainty.

Silence fell between them because Sammer knew that they'd know when they knew.

Phase 3

As best Sammer could reconstruct, what happened last 4th of July was based on the words of a single-eyed witness (with an eyepatch no less!), Misty Spigal.

She didn't really have one eye, but she suffered from a lazy crossed eye, hence the eye-patch, which her moribund mother made her wear because the patch made Misty single-minded.

Misty always said the same thing over-and-over when Sammer asked her. "It's so horrible I don't never-ever want to talk about it—not even for money." But, while down in the sewer pipe one afternoon, Misty persuaded Sammer to kiss her once on the lips and then, afterwards, without prompting, told him all she had seen.

Misty Spigal couldn't see too good but the cross-eyed girl was a fabstoryteller—even Screech had to admit it. Sammer didn't even have time to stick his fingers in his ears and his asthma started up even before Misty finished.

Misty Spigal said Screech's father took the four-wheeler out for what was to be a trip up to Arbuckle Hill to trim the wild rose bushes he loved so much. Until that day, Screech thought it "Silly for a grown man to want to trim rose bushes without the prodding of some naggin' woman," but Screech's father loved those wild rose bushes and treated them with the care homeless men give to the whelp of their shoes.

"Screech's father," Misty said, "jumpedjumpedjumped on top the four-wheeler without the helmet he had always forced Screech to wear. He had alwaysalwaysalways been such a careful man," Misty Spigal said, "about 40 minutes later," she "saw (and mind you what she saw was blurry) Screech's father walking back down the road holding a bouquet of wild roses with blood spouting like the Three Rivers' Fountain out of his head.

"And, Screech's Daddy was talking non-stop about the wild-roses the whole time he was walking, and he kept talkingtalkingtalkingtalking long after Screech's mamma screamed and Screech called 911.

"The paramedics didn't let Screech's mamma ride in the ambulance to Pass-Away Hospital. Screech suggested they take the other four-wheeler, and after Screech said it, Screech's Mamma smacked Screech hard on the head and said loudly that she felt bad about doing it but Screech deserved it."

It looked for a week or so like Screech's father was going to make it. It really did "to all and everyoneandeverybody concerned"—that's the way Misty Spigal said it because she read a lot.

Misty told Sammer that she used to take the big Shakespeare book to the Peoples Elementary School bathroom as her bathroom pass instead of the wooden key paddle Mr. Stock, the Language Arts teacher, made them drag down to the toilets, and there was probably a story in that, too, but it wasn't this story she said—it wasn't this story at all.

"Each and every day," Misty Spigal said, "Screech brought them pinking shears to the hospital—hiding them under his black T's so that his daddy might work-workwork them if he ever woke up.

"Then, he did wake up, but his speech was all a jumbled and the words came out wrongwrongwrong— lots of mean-spirited words," Misty Spigal said, "sounded like Lucifer had got into his tonsils!"

"Screeches' father would say these badbadbad words as he workworkworked the pinking shears cutting the imaginary wild rose bushes."

Then, Misty Spigal said, "The crazy spasms started, and the hospital orderlies had to take Screech and his mama away because seeing the convulsions would permanently damage their mind's eye."

Misty Spigal adjusted her eye patch. "The first time

Screech saw them convulsions, his father had been holding the pinking shears and nearly cut off his little finger."

"Mercifully," Misty Spigal said, Screech's father slipped permanently into deep blue unconsciousness for the better part of a week, and they all—Screech and his mama, focused every attention and all of their prayers on the blips that came out the machines.

"They kept vigil on the OXYGEN. One monitor kept increasing intake and the other kept decreasing until at 7 AM on July 4th, nearly one week after the accident, Screech's father took his very last breath.

Screech put the pinking shears in the casket after cutting a lock of his father's hair, and he's been attending to the wild roses ever since, but he's got to walk all the way up Mon-hill because his mamma won't let him anywhere near that four-wheeler, even with the promise to wear a helmet.

Phase 4

Screech's Daddy was not a showy man, and he wanted to be buried in a pine box and even wrote instructions in his hand-scrawled will to that effect, but the Arbuckle Hill mortician, Mr. Pupillary, said they didn't bury people in pine boxes no more.

Screech's Mamma didn't fight Mr. Pupillary; instead, she bought that big metal barge, made out of steel from the mill he used to work in, and there in their family plot atop Arbuckle Hill, he lay forever, probably swearing to high Heaven to let him out of the steel coffin.

"There it is, Zion," Screech said and pointed to the concrete tombstones and wooden crosses that stuck up out the ground peeking through the smoke and fog. They made their way through row after row as if looking for the switch in familiar rooms.

THE BIG SUCKER was surprisingly light.

"Be sure to tie her down tight. We don't want this sucker to fly off sideways and find its way through the windshield of an ambulating vehicle."

"FUGGIN' CLOUDS. This was not how I imagined it!"

In a better universe, Screech's words would have, upon command, caused the clouds to part, and then they could point THE BIG SUCKER at the moons of Jupiter. But, tonight the smoky clouds were so heavy that Sammer felt as if he were standing in the middle of a soupy rain.

"SHOULD WE LIGHT THE SUCKER?"

Sammer was again silent while Screech found the fuse.

"I want to see the world explode," Screech said. "I want to see it pull apart so even God can't put the egg together again! Nothin' turns out the way you see it, so let this be a launch of faith."

Screech reached into his pocket.

"Zippo ain't let me down yet."

Screech lit the fuse. Silently they mounted THE BIG SUCKER to his Pop's tombstone cross and made sure it was pointing straight up.

Sammer and Screech moved a good distance away

behind the Anderson's Concrete Ink Pot—a solid enough structure, they figured. The fuse curled up as it steamed toward THE BIG SUCKER, caught wildly, and then went dead out a few inches from the rocket.

"FUG!FUG!FUG!FUG! Damned to hell, I am."

Screech pinched the fuse still attached to THE BIG SUCKER between his fingers to make sure that it was no longer lit. Then, checked the strap, careful to keep his body between Sammer to shield what he was doing.

"Don't get your panties in a bunch, an at!"

"Just checkin!"

Screech's fingers fumbled with the Zippo. "Pop? You ready?"

There just wouldn't be enough time to light it and get behind Anderson's Concrete Ink Pot.

"Nothing should take so long. Why does everything take so Fuggin' long?"

Screech's fingers kept working, snapping the Zippo over the fuse, which wouldn't light.

Sammer's hands began to sweat, and in his mind's eye, he saw himself rushing in before Screech blew off his head, snatching the fuse, leaving Screech and the Rusted Red to face the sadness that was himself.

Then, they would wait for a proper 4th—maybe next year, maybe the next.

Screeches' daddy could yell like the Dickens for another year in his metal coffin. What was another year for dead?

They could hide the BIG SUCKER upstairs in the 333 —pay Straight 50 to keep it covered with a tarp.

The old codger would do it. He'd do it for Screech's

father. He'd say, "'*There was a barren field; a place abhorr'd /For it was there where wretched criminals / Were done to die; and there they built the stake, / And piled the fuel round, that should consume / The accused Maid, abandon'd, as it seem'd, / By God and Man.*'"[3]

Either Screech would or wouldn't get over it. It didn't matter. And if he did get over it, they would still both be better for it, even if they weren't friends anymore.

They would climb Mon-hill together again; sure they would; the sky would be clear and would be lit by the moon and together they would secure THE BIG SUCKER to Screech's father's cross and maybe even light it together.

Then, they would run and hide behind Anderson's Concrete Ink Pot and turn around together just in time to watch THE BIG SUCKER screech a red streak toward the moons of Jupiter, continuing upupup.

"You better get away from that fuse, Sammer, or you'll force me to kick your ever-smiling ass."

Sammer reached for his inhaler. Sammer's daddy told Sammer that without access to his medicine he could die. Sammer was not as afraid of asthma death, as he was of losing his best friend.

"Looklooklook and see what a pile of shit life puts in your palm," Screech said holding the short fuse between his fingertips still trying to light it. "Sammer, I know you're faking it. Fuggin' convenient ashma."

Screech got down on his knees and kept his ear to the ground. "Stop yelling your head off, Pop! I'll make that barge into a pine box yet if it's the fuggin end of us."

The world should stop, at least for a moment. That's

what Sammer thought, but unfortunately, the world was not listening.

"I hear you yelling, Pops. I hear you," Screech said and lit what was left of the fuse and yelled "BOOM!" when it burned down to his skin.

Even as Screech finished mouthing these last words, Sammer recognized in them an irrevocable sadness that never allowed for "do-overs," even if you had the presence to hold onto a moment and stop the world from hurling toward the unknown.

Sammer wasn't listening, though. He had his fingers pressed very deep inside his ears.

Phase 5

Through the doorless doorway of the 333, Kind Annie, Ben Birthright, TOMMY 25 and Straight 50 saw the rocket light up the July 4th night.

"No shit, that's a big ass firecracker en at," TOMMY 25 said.

"The BIG FUCKER!" Ben Birthright said.

"SUCKER!" Kind Annie said.

The rocket rose straight and true up from Arbuckle

Hill Cemetery, where Straight 50 used to throw baseballs in the summer.

There were still crosses up there, he'd be willing to bet, with pockmarks on 'em. The crosses were the same size as the sweet, soft spot in a catcher's mitt.

"Better than the finale," Kind Annie said.

"Super loud, too," Ben Birthright said.

Straight 50 thrust his hand into the pickled egg jar, and it pricked suddenly as if his finger had caught on a thorn.

Had they known his pitching practice regimen, the nuns surely would have taken a ruler to Straight 50's pitchin' knuckles and then made him recite in the Nun's Poetry Corner,

"'*They rose, they spread, they raged— / The breath of God went forth; the ascending fire / Beneath its influence bent, and all its flames / In one long lightning flash collecting fierce, / ...Now first beheld since Paradise was lost, / And fill with Eden odours all the air.*' "[4]

THE LAST TELEGRAPH

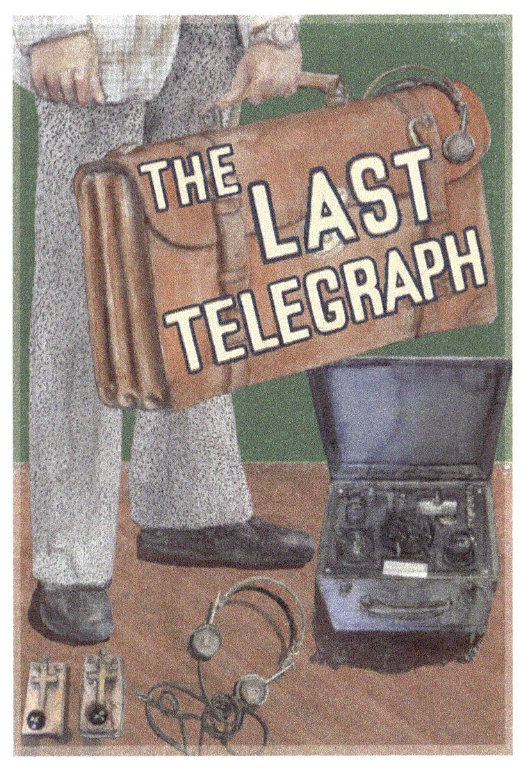

I was a regular Chatty-William until I was ten—a wailing dervish, running around the house, my voice full-throttle, scaling up throughout the day, the pitch increasing at an ever-alarming rate.

My mother, on the advice of a slew of throat specialists, purchased a clicker in an attempt to quiet me. She clicked once for each word.

In perpetual motion through the turbulent channels of life—I spewed schwas, sputtered fricatives, and even made my own clicks, which confounded my mother.

As the day wore on, I amplified vowels, consonants, affixes, words, phrases, and finally whole sentences until, by mid-afternoon, my voice had transmogrified into high-squealing frequencies, unnerving in duration —louder, louder, louder still.

My desire to be heard, to be noticed, to be understood, produced in listeners the very opposite of its intended effect.

Mother's neighbors: Uncle Vail, Miss Sturgeon, and Mister Gale graced our summer afternoons. At first, they'd given me audience, pushing kitchen chairs into the living room's center, attending to me and attempting to make sense of my formant transitions. No luck. After five minutes, they'd push their index fingers deep into their ears, their eyes still following me in an attempt to identify my segmented speech streams.

Suburban decorum suggested they wait long enough for a semblance of a proper visit: Upon completion of a cup of tea and a sugar cookie, these overly polite neighbors would suddenly bolt from our midst without a real excuse—although they would stammer through many—vowing that there was a grave matter they must attend.

After they'd taken leave, I continued through the frequency spectrum: shrieking, wailing, and yelling until sometime in the late afternoon, my voice would STOP. After that, I emitted only a throbbing unvoiced hiss like a broken steam-heater, and had I stood next to one, I'm certain I'd have felt the need to compete with it until my hissing overwhelmed it.

Late in the afternoon, my father, with briefcase in hand—an accordion box that was filled with what felt like rocks—made headway into the late-light of our recently vacated living room, and set down his heavy load. My mother showed my father the tally on the clicker, and he'd shake his head and unburden himself of his tie, which he'd hang in a twisted mess on a single wire hanger in the hall closet.

Then, he'd point at me and toward the downstairs bathroom. Dutifully, with a bar of soap, I'd wash my dirty hands, and subsequently find my way to the kitchen table, pull up a chair, and sit down to a dinner my mother had somehow prepared between the time the neighbors had left and my father had found himself in our midst. Spoons, forks, and knives clattered—my parents undoubtedly thankful for what in our house resembled silence.

In that we owned no television set—my father referred to TV as "the idiot box"—after dinner, he'd push back his chair with a scrape, and together we'd find our way into his "den"—a very square room near the back of the house.

While standing in front of the waist-high white bookshelves on the den's far end, he would remove a book with his thimble-thick fingers and point to the ancient telegraph machine that sat alone on what we called our "ship table"— a varnished door, impossibly heavy that held gold and silver medallions fuzzily visible underneath its shellacked veneer. I imagined the coins were worth a great amount of money and ignored the shellac's stalactite drips that gave me pause.

Together, we would sit side-by-side on a straight-back hard pew-of-a-workbench in front of the old telegraph machine and its ancient telegraph key and spool.

My father would open the book he'd selected to a random page: Stevenson, Dickens, Twain, or Faulkner, say, "The past is not dead. It's not even past." I'd work out the Morse code, and he'd let me tap it into the machine and send it off.

Then, we'd put on headphones, eye the large metal wheel that spooled the ticker tape, and wait. The waiting was the delicious part—an anticipation of a response from the future or the past.

During the pause, I could barely sit still, although I'd trained myself to do just that. And even if, throat willing, I could have said something, I'm not sure what it would have been. Usually, I had little trouble conjuring words and found the meaning of the sentences that followed the second they came out of me, but within the silent walls of my father's den, I tried to imagine what I might say if I had been able, but the words just wouldn't present themselves.

Miraculously, however, the telegraph's ticker-wheel

broke the silence and began to turn, its needle making dots and dashes while my father translated responses.

He wrote out each reply's translation for me to check against tape: "Every child has a dream, to pursue the dream is in every child's hand to make it a reality. One's invention is another's tool."[1]

"...One's invention is another's tool." I couldn't figure that one out for the life of me, but it sounded pretty and seemed to be saying something about the present and the future: How one thing leads to another. And as my father watched me pore over the words, making sure he had correctly decoded them, I imagine that he wondered: Who is this creature, this boy, William Alexander, who refuses to remain silent until forced into it. Who refuses to listen, except to the last telegraph machine?

The tape continued to tick, and my father would write out a translation and again give it to me to check against the tape: "The great object of human thought is the discovery of truth or, in other words, to arrive at conceptions and expressions of things which shall agree with the nature of things."[2]

The second phrase was clearly about truth, but I didn't know what the nature of things was. What things? Was it in my nature to yell my throat closed each afternoon? Was I bound forever to spend time in silence with my father? Was this how we were destined to communicate? Through the quotations he read and the responses we received from others? These were truths, yes, but not our own words. And I wondered where our own words had gone.

And unlike a photograph or even his storied voice,

my father's handwriting, whenever I see it, even now, conjures him up for me. Takes me to a place beyond his voice—lets me into his essential core—that unchanging part of us all that remains constant throughout our lives.

My mother always used to say, when she showed the clicker to my father and he wearily shook his head, "It is what it is." I hated that sentence, refused to believe any part of it—within those words, there was no room for possibility.

After I'd double-check the ticker's responses, my father would read them aloud. When he received nothing from me but silence, he'd shut the machine off, it's winding reel slowing to a stop; and after unplugging it, and handing me the ticker tape, he'd say something like: "All knowledge is profitable; profitable in its ennobling effect on the character, in the pleasure it imparts in its acquisition, as well as in the power it gives over the operations of mind and of matter"[3]—all those plosives that swam that night through my dreams.

The world ends up taking funny turns; it just does, and I'm convinced that whoever or whatever has put it together finds ways to slowly take away what it is that one loves, and this leads to the gradual abandonment of desire.

One morning toward the beginning of August, the tenor, the pitch, the rate of my speech increased suddenly, and then gave out so completely it dissolved from a hiss to a rasp and then stopped in mid-click right in front of the neighbors. They sat in those hard-backed kitchen chairs in stone silence, and as I stood in front of them. I sounded less like a broken steam heater than a fish gasping for air. They didn't leave this time, but oddly began voicing thoughts as if I couldn't have heard them. "I think he's run out of electricity," Uncle Vale said. "I think he's finally broken," Miss Sturgeon replied. "Perhaps this is the end of that terrible voiced machine inside of him," Mister Gale said.

That evening, while we sat at the dinner table, my mother and father discussed "the situation" in front of me as if I wasn't there. Both were certain, they said as they eyed one another with reassuring glances that my squalling, my squealing, my squawking would return the next morning.

But the next morning, my throat had closed almost completely, and, without a vehicle to call attention to myself, I began to believe there was absolutely nothing left of me. I was struggling to breathe, and whenever I tried to communicate, I turned very red in the face.

Perhaps because of the sudden change, Uncle Vail, Miss Sturgeon, and Mister Gale paid full attention to the silence that was me.

As for my part, I began to believe that by being silent, I was re-creating the world. The neighbors watched my gesticulations intently, parceling me out as my body literally turned and twisted into letters: Miss Sturgeon decoded each of the consonants; Uncle Vail sounded out the vowels; Mister Gale wrote it all down in a flip-top notebook. They waited, they watched my body turn into lettered shapes and called out: I/ have/ never/ had/ my/ admiration/ of/ any/ man/ increased/ by/ reading/ his/life[4]. I reveled in their attention and began to believe I was creating and re-creating the world.

As the day wore into afternoon, the neighbors became more practiced at decoding me: Uncle Vale became adept with subtext; Miss Sturgeon with implicature; Mister Gale with the pragmatics of movement. And as I moved, I became my father, carefully selecting passages and embodying them. "There is a fellowship more quiet even than solitude, and which, rightly understood, is solitude made perfect," from Robert Lewis Stevenson for Uncle Vale, who unburdened himself of his handkerchief, decoded the quotation on it, and wiped his face blue. "What I wanted, who can say? How can I say, when I never knew?" from Dickens for Mister Gale, who wrote down the letters on his hand and looked longingly at Miss Sturgeon, who I then realized was his Estella, and the primary reason he adorned our living room was to be close to her. And "I felt so lonesome I most wished I was dead" from Huck Finn. This, I hoped the neighbors understood, was irony, which my father said was the highest form of intelligence.

Then the world paused: my father interrupted us, having come home from work early. In slow motion, we watched as he unburdened himself of his accordion briefcase and, in front of us all, attempted to untie his tie but instead fell into the couch that held his imprint.

From a short distance away, I waited for him to acknowledge me, but my mother appeared at his side, hesitantly, with a glass of water. At that moment, I hoped for a kind of reversal—I hoped the real alphabet would spill out of me.

Instead, I watched my father silently hold out his hand for the water glass that my mother might well have forgotten she was holding. Without opening his eyes, he gulped down the liquid. My mother motioned me into the kitchen to fetch another glass of water. No words passed her lips.

While I was in the midst of filling up another glass, my mother emitted a loud animal screech whose sound moved around the living room and silenced the dazed neighbors. I raced back, my hands dripping. My father lay in nearly the same position, emitting a kind of hissing —which soon morphed into a clicking. Dot dot dash/dot dash dot/dot dot/dot/ dash dot dot.

Miss Sturgeon placed her cold, dry hands against my throat, looked searchingly into my eyes, and whispered, "Silence." Uncle Vale held me firmly by the shoulders and said, "Stillness." Mister Gale put the tip of his index finger on the crown of my head, wound me up, and then allowed the other two to spin me around like a top until I unraveled, and he said, "You're healed, speak."

I raced down the hall toward my father's den, grabbed the telegraph, and ran back into the living room. I read the quotation my father had last selected: Samuel Morse's initial message when demonstrating the first telegraph: "What Hath God Wrought."[5]

And for the first time that day the house was truly silent and for one final time the old telegraph machine sputtered, its tape unspooling a series of dots and dashes and I heard clearly my father's voice translate the text: "All parts of the material universe are in constant motion and though some of the changes may appear to be cyclical, nothing ever exactly returns, so far as human experience extends, to precisely the same condition."[6]

NOTES

THE BANKRUPT CIRCUS

1. Thomas Sowell, "Random thoughts on the passing scene," *Deseret News*, October 6, 2005

INNOCENTLY TO AMUSE
THE IMAGINATION IN THIS
DREAM OF LIFE IS WISDOM

1. G.K. Chesterton, "Why I Am a Catholic," *Twelve Modern Apostles and Their Creeds* (1926)

2. Thomas De Quincey, *Confessions of an English Opium-Eater* (1821)

3. Michel de Montaigne, "Of Friendship," *Essays* (1580) (adapted)

4. William Hazlitt, "On the Past and Future," *Table-Talk: Essays on Men and Manners* (1821)

5. Ralph Waldo Emerson, "Character," *Lectures and Biographical Sketches* (1883)

6. Anonymous (often misattributed to Mark Twain)

7. Ralph Waldo Emerson, "Eloquence," *Society and Solitude* (1870)

8. Virginia Woolf, *The Waves* (1931)

9. Virginia Woolf (attributed)

10. Virginia Woolf, *A Room of One's Own* (1929)

11. William Hazlitt, *The Round Table* (1817)

12. Thomas De Quincey, *Confessions of an English Opium-Eater* (1821)

13. Ralph Waldo Emerson, "Spiritual Laws," *Essays: First Series* (1841)

14. William Hazlitt, "Thoughts on Taste," *Edinburgh Magazine* (1818)

15. G.K. Chesterton, "Folly and Female Education," *What's Wrong with the World* (1910)

16. G.K. Chesterton, *St. Francis of Assisi* (1923)

17. George Santayana, *The Life of Reason: Reason in Common Sense*, Volume 1 (1905)

18. Kurt Vonnegut, *Slaughterhouse-Five* (1969)

19. John Milton, "Il Penseroso" (1631)

20. Ralph Waldo Emerson, "Nature" (1836)

21. Mark Twain, *What Is Man?* (1906)

22. Jean-Jacques Rousseau, *The Social Contract* (1762)

23. Henry David Thoreau, Journal (March 12, 1842)

24. G.K. Chesterton (attributed)

25. Samuel Johnson, *The Adventurer*, No. 84 (August 25, 1753)

26. Marcus Tullius Cicero (attributed)

27. William Hazlitt, "On Poetry in General," *Lectures on the English Poets* (1818)

28. William Hazlitt, "On Poetry in General," *Lectures on the English Poets* (1818)

29. William Hazlitt, "On Poetry in General," *Lectures on the English Poets* (1818)

30. William Hazlitt, "On Poetry in General," *Lectures on the English Poets* (1818)

31. Mark Twain (attributed)

32. Ralph Waldo Emerson, *Journals* (1909 edition)

33. William Hazlitt (attributed)

34. G.K. Chesterton, "The Flag of the World," *Orthodoxy* (1908)

35. Samuel Johnson (attributed)

36. Mark Twain, *Following the Equator* (1897), Chapter 39

37. W.B. Yeats, *Essays* (1924), page 423

SCREECH AND THE
DARK-SHIRTED STREETS

1. Robert Southey, *The Rose* (1798)

2. Robert Southey, *The Rose* (1798)

3. Robert Southey, *The Rose* (1798)

4. Robert Southey, *The Rose* (1798)

THE LAST TELEGRAPH

1. Samuel Morse.

2. Joseph Henry lecture on geology and revelation.

3. Joseph Henry in 'Report of the Secretary', Sixth Annual Report of the Board of Regents of the Smithsonian Institution for 1851.

4. Joseph Henry Letter to Alexander Dallas Bache, July 31, 1855, in Henry Papers, vol. 9, p. 271.

5. The text of Samuel Morse's demonstration message, "What Hath God Wrought," came from the Bible, Numbers.
6. Joseph Henry Address (Jul 1874) at the grave of Joseph Priestley.

Acknowledgments

In *The Poetics of Space*, Gaston Bachelard suggests that in one's first house is intimacy: From the barely lit basement, whose very walls bulge and push against the earth to the vaulted attic, whose joists and joints are constant reminders of the structure's architecture, craft, workmanship and space. Thus, when examining a completed project, one must ask who has brought this space—this first house— into existence? Alas, there were many who helped put up these tents and whose hands helped *The Bankrupt Circus & Other Misadventures* find solvency.

I'd like to thank the amazing John Jarrett, the publisher of Silent Clamor Press, whose undaunted enthusiasm and tireless work ethic helped to dream this book into existence. John you have made this one of the most memorable acts in my life.

I'd like to thank my beautiful wife, story editor extraordinaire, Mary Ellen Kubit, who has juggled each of these misadventures and has been careful not to let any one of them fall to the ground. That you keep trying is my inspiration.

Thank you to my spiritual brother (of a different mother) Johnny Payne, who has taught me how to shoot myself out of a writing cannon and to fly in a generally upward direction.

Thank you to my fallen brothers, who have taught me to walk the tightrope of time: Michael Kleine, William E. Coles, Jr., Jim Levernier, Ben Fry, and Mark Spitzer. Your memory inhabits these stories.

I'd like to thank the editors of the following stupendous literary journals and magazines who first published these stories (sometimes in a slightly different forms): "The Bankrupt Circus" in *Cleaver*. "Innocently to Amuse the Imagination in this Dream of Life is Wisdom" in *East of the Web*. "No One Beats Vitas Gerulaitis 17 Times in a Row" in *The GroundUp*. "Generative/Iterative/ Evaluative," "Clean-up in the Meat Department," Working The Dirt," and "A Pebble At Dawn" in *Literally Stories*. "Screech and The Dark-Shirted Streets" in *Lit Bop: Art and Literature in the Groove*. "The Last Telegraph" in *St. Katherine Review*. And "The Twisted S" in *Twelve Winters Journal*.

Thank you to the superlative writers who supplied blurbs: Kevin Brockmeier, Robert Olin Butler, William Lychack, Jo McDougall, Stewart O'Nan, Johnny Payne, and John Vanderslice.

I'd especially like to thank the wise and wonderful Karen Rile, founding editor of *Cleaver Magazine,* who created the cover illustration and the interior illustration for "The Bankrupt Circus." I'd like to thank the brave, kind and thought-filled Ryan Scribner, publisher of *The GroundUp* for the illustration for the story "Nobody Beats Vitas Gerulaitis 17 Times in a Row." And, I'd especially like to thank the incomparable artist and illustrator LK Sukany for her partnership, her talent, her imagination, her inspiration, her faith and for all of the other illustrations in this book.

A special thanks to Jeff Sewald and Frank Thurmond for always being there.

I'd like to thank my longtime friends: Sean Andrews, Jennifer Brown, Sam Brown, Ezra Cappell, John Dunn, Joseph Fuller, Jeremy Graeff, Sam Gregory, Chris Hausammann, Michael Hibblen, Chris Hickey, Silas Hite, Bill Kerns, Spencer Kenney, Chip Meister, Ken Morris, Brian Nahlen, Mark Nelson, Trey Philpotts, Lauren Pifer, Dan Reimer, Mike Reimer, Karen Rissling, Adam Simon, William Wagner, Erick Weed, Kara and Jesse Wells.

I'd like to thank all my colleagues and dear friends in the UA Little Rock English Program (Paul Crutcher, Jeff Condran, Jeremy Ecke, Heather Hummel, Angela Hunter, Kris McAbee, Frank Thurmond, Laura Barrio Vilar) and everyone at UA Little Rock. I'd like to thank all those at The University of Pittsburgh, including William Lychack and Anthony Petrosky. I'd like to thank all those at the University of Texas at El Paso, including Keith Polette and Tony Stafford.

A special thank you to Stephen Koziol, my mentor and second father.

I'd like to thank my brilliant sister Lynn Ann Minnick, my mother, Mary Dunham Minnick, and my dear departed dad, Daniel Robert Minnick. As you can see by the portraitures on the dedication page, this one was for you Mom and Dad.

I'd like to thank anyone and everyone I've forgotten

to mention: friends, students, teachers, colleagues and associates and ask humbly for your forgiveness.

The *Bankrupt Circus & Other Misadventures* has evolved over four decades. In these circus tents, I have striven to build intimate structures out of these character's lives. Like them I will keep dreaming; I will keep imagining; and, I will keep trying until the tiny wheels fall away and the tents are taken down, only to be put up in another town.

STEP RIGHT UP, FOLKS AND PEEK INSIDE.

ILLUSTRATOR BIOGRAPHIES

Karen Rile is the founding editor and resident illustrator for the literary magazine *Cleaver,* and teaches in the writing program at the University of Pennsylvania. She is the author of Winter Music (Little, Brown), a novel set in Philadelphia, and numerous short works of fiction and creative nonfiction. Read her essays on human bodies at the intersection of literature and politics on her Substack, Embodied Resistance.

Ryan Scribner is the publisher of The GroundUp and he is wrapping up edits of his second novel.

L.K. Sukany is a multimedia artist, illustrator, singer, and songwriter. Her band, the Damsels in Distress, just released its seventh album, *Hey!,* in May 2025. Sukany has been exhibiting art for over 25 years, and illustrating for publications. She lives with her husband and five children in a large, but snug shoe somewhere in Southern suburbia USA. She can be found on paper-opera.com.

ABOUT THE AUTHOR

(photo credit: M.E. Kubit)

J. Bradley Minnick is a writer, public radio host and producer, and a Professor of English at the University of Arkansas at Little Rock. He has written, edited, and produced the one-minute spot "Facts About Fiction," and the award-winning program Arts & Letters Radio, a show celebrating modern humanities with a concentration on Southern cultural and intellectual work that can be streamed at artsandlettersradio.org. He has published fiction in *Toad Suck Review, Burningword Literary Journal, Literally Stories, Inklette Magazine, Cleaver, Twelve Winters*

Journal, East of the Web, Litbop Art and Literature in the Groove, Rural Fiction Magazine, Café Lit, Potato Soup Journal's 'Best of 2022' anthology, and Southwest Review. He spends his time with his amazing wife in Little Rock, Southwest Virginia and Pittsburgh.

At Silent Clamor Press, we seek to illuminate the human experience with excitement, elegance, and unflinching honesty. If this work has resonated with you—offering a profound journey or a new way of seeing the world—consider sharing your reflections with others. Your voice enriches the ongoing conversation that keeps literature vital and transformative.

www.ingramcontent.com/pod-product-compliance
Lightning Source LLC
Chambersburg PA
CBHW061122100726
47911CB00013B/649